HARDIN'S STAND

by

Jacquelyn Bishop

1

For Sarah Wegner
My first friend, my truest friend.
From childhood days filled with laughter and scraped
knees
to quiet moments and deep conversations across the
years—
your presence has been a constant light.
This story, like so many of our own, is stitched with
loyalty, courage, and heart.
Thank you for walking beside me through every chapter.

With love, always.

Table of Contents

PROLOGUE

The sun baked the main street of Copper Creek until the boards creaked and the air shimmered. It was the kind of heat that pressed on a man, heavy and merciless. Doors hung half-open, shutters sagged, and the only movement came from a stray dog nosing through the street.

The town itself seemed to wilt beneath it, tired of the long drought and tired of the long shadow cast by one man's name: Jed Crowe.

The sound of hoofbeats echoed slow and steady, and heads turned. The heat shimmered over the wide main street of Copper Creek as a tall figure rode slowly into town. His hat brim shadowed a pair of steady blue eyes, and the creak of his saddle was the only sound besides the restless whine of the wind. Folks paused in their doings—the blacksmith lowering his hammer, the saloon girl paused in the doorway, a boy stood holding a bucket of water too heavy for his arms, and even the boy with a stick stopped chasing tumbleweed to stare at the stranger. They didn't know him, but they could feel it: this was a man who belonged anywhere he set foot.

The lone rider came into town, tall in the saddle, shoulders broad as the horizon. His horse, a rangy buckskin, moved steady beneath him, hooves clicking against the hard-packed earth. He rode with no hurry, no wasted motion, as if the land itself moved aside to let him pass.

A quiet fell as he passed— a shopkeeper who stopped sweeping his porch, then two boys who lowered their slingshots, then a pair of gamblers drifting out of the saloon.

The stranger's presence carried weight. The cut of his shoulders, the calm in his eyes, and the way he sat his horse told folks more than words ever could.

Swinging open the batwing doors of the saloon, stepped a broad-shouldered man with a cruel grin and a black hat pulled low. His boots struck the boards like gunshots. Everyone knew him: Jed Crowe, the man who owned Copper Creek by fear alone.

"Well now." Crowe spat into the dust, a smirk tugging at his scarred cheek. "Looks like we got ourselves a visitor," he drawled, voice carrying loud enough for every ear. "Hope you know how to mind your own business, stranger. A big fella like you don't just pass through. You aim to try and make Copper Creek your business?"

The rider dismounted, his shadow long across the street. He tied his reins to the hitching post, straightened, and looked Crowe dead in the eye. His voice was deep, calm, steady as bedrock.

"My business," he said, "is seeing men like you don't own what don't belong to 'em." He touched his finger to his hat at said, "Name's Cole Hardin."

A hush swept the street. The townsfolk froze, hearts thudding, while the hot wind rattled a loose shutter. Crowe's grin faltered just a fraction, and in that heartbeat, everyone knew—trouble had finally come to Copper Creek, and this time it had a name.

CHAPTER ONE:
A Stranger in Copper Creek

His bay gelding's hooves drummed hollow on the packed dirt as eyes peered out from half-drawn shutters.

Cole Hardin swung down outside the livery stable, boots sinking in dust. The air smelled of hay and horse sweat. A boy of about fifteen scurried from the shadows, wiping his nose on his sleeve.

"You'll be wantin 'me to see to him, mister?"

Cole handed over the reins and a coin. "Bay's name is Ace. Rub him down good, keep his water clean. He's steady, but don't get behind him unless you like flyin'."

The boy's eyes went around, but his grin spread quick. "Yes, sir! I'll see him right."

Cole gave the horse a last pat, then pulled his saddlebags over his shoulder. "Where does a man get a room in this town?"

The boy's smile faltered. "Boardin 'house. Widow Hensley runs it, two streets over." He shifted nervously. "But… folks don't like takin 'sides these days. You stay too long, Crowe'll notice."

Cole adjusted his hat, his voice low and flat. "Reckon I'm already noticed."

* * *

He turned up Main Street, the town unfolding around him: the shuttered barber's shop, the empty porch of the saloon where a piano sat mute, the faded sign of the telegraph office.

He walked on. Caldwell's General Store stood near the center of town, windows shaded by sun-bleached curtains. He pushed the door open, and a small bell jingled.

Inside, the air was cooler, smelling of flour, leather, and kerosene. Dust swirled in the sunlight pouring through the front windows, and every eye in the room shifted his way.

Behind the counter stood Maggie Caldwell, her dark hair streaked with silver and tied back, her sleeves rolled up to her elbows. Her ledger lay open, her twelve-year-old son, Jesse, perched on a flour barrel, chewing licorice like it was the only sweet thing left in the world.

"You're new," Maggie said, sharp-eyed, sizing him up. "And tall enough to block my light if you don't step aside."

Cole tipped his hat and stepped aside, that crooked grin of his never wavering. "Name's Cole Hardin. Reckon I could use some coffee, tobacco, and cartridges, if you've got 'em."

"Sell it all, if a man can pay."

He nodded, and she gathered his things off the shelves. Her hands were steady as she wrapped the goods, but her voice dropped low. "Just a warnin', mister. Be careful. Men who cross Crowe don't last long in Copper Creek."

Cole looked at her, calm and steady. "I didn't come here to last long. Just came to do right."

Her lips pressed tight. She slid the bundle across the counter. "Then God help you."

The bell above the door clanged again. Three of Crowe's men swaggered in, spurs jangling, laughter oily. One kicked a crate aside as if to remind the room who owned the place. Another pushed past Cole deliberately, brushing his shoulder.

"Well, well," the first one sneered, looking Cole up and down, "a new rooster strutting' the yard." Then he turned to Maggie, eyeing her." And, looky here," one drawled. He jabbed a dirty finger at the candy jar. "Gimme that, sweetheart. On the house."

Maggie didn't flinch. She slammed the jar down on the counter so hard the lid popped. "Pay for it, or choke on it."

Jesse hopped down, fire in his eyes. "Ain't nothing free in this store."

The thug's grin widened as he reached for the boy. But a large hand clamped down on his wrist — Cole's.

"Best not," Cole said, low and steady.

The room went still. Then the other two lunged. Cole moved fast — one punch flattened a nose, another man went crashing into a stack of molasses jars that burst in sticky brown rain. Jesse whooped, grabbing a broom handle and swinging wild. Maggie vaulted the counter, grabbing a broom and cracking the nearest thug across the skull with a clean, sharp blow. She jabbed her broom square across the third's nose with a satisfying crack, sending him staggering into a stack of canned peaches.

At the doorway stood Sheriff Silas Boone. He was tall once, still broad, but his shoulders had folded in like a man who carried a weight he couldn't shake. His badge hung crooked and dull on his vest. He'd arrived too late, as always.

"Enough," Boone said, voice heavy with weariness, his face lined with fear. He had once been a strong man, but Crowe's reign had hollowed him out. His voice shook as he raised his hands. "Put the guns away, boys. No need for blood on a hot day."

Deke smirked, but he and the others backed off, not out of respect for the law, but because Crowe hadn't given the word yet.

"Crowe's men don't need more reason to raise hell. And you, stranger — best ride on while you can," he sheriff warned.

Cole met the sheriff's eye. "I'll ride when I'm ready."

Jesse spat on the floor. "Some sheriff you are. Always warnin', never stoppin'."

Boone's jaw tightened, but he said nothing.

"Out!" Maggie roared, chasing them toward the door, broom swinging like a saber. Cole cuffed the last one across the jaw for good measure, booting him into the street. The men scrambled off, cursing and covered in sugar and syrup, bloodied and humiliated.

Silence settled, broken only by Jesse's snickering. He picked up a dented tin of peaches and held it up like a trophy. "That was the best fight this store's seen all week. "

Cole tipped his hat to Maggie. "You can add a broom to my order — it seems you broke yours."

Maggie's lips twitched despite herself. "The broom's on the house. Don't think that makes you special, Hardin."

Sheriff Boone lingered by the door, eyes shadowed. "You've made yourself a mark, Hardin. Crowe won't let this stand." Boone shook his head. The sheriff's voice was heavy as the dust that never seemed to settle. "You don't know Crowe," he said, turning away. "This town belongs to him. Always has."

And with that, Silas Boone walked out into the rising heat, shoulders bent, leaving the silence thick behind him.

Cole leaned against the counter, brushing dust from his sleeve. "You run a lively shop, Miss Caldwell. You always sweep customers out that hard?"

She smirked, brushing a loose strand of hair back with her wrist. "Only the ones who won't pay."

Maggie planted the broom handle on the floor, cheeks flushed but eyes sharp. "And I intend to keep it that way."

"Ma, he beat 'em! He walloped every one of 'em!" Jesse smirked, stuffing another licorice stick between his teeth. "Next time, Mr. Hardin, maybe you'll let me throw the first punch."

Cole crouched down, resting a hand on the lad's shoulder. "Easy now, son. A fight's not something to crow about." He shot the boy a wink. "Still, reckon they won't be bothering your ma for a while."

14

But Maggie's smirk faded as quick as it had come. She leaned across the counter, lowering her voice. "You don't know Jed Crowe. Humiliatin 'his men in front of the whole town? That's not something he forgives."

Cole straightened, his expression calm, steady. "Then I'll be ready when he comes."

Cole gave her the faintest of smiles, then stepped back into the morning glare. A shadow fell across the street. Crowe's men leaned against the hitching post, watching him. Deke Slater, Crowe's right-hand man— spat a stream of tobacco juice and grinned mean.

"You're a tall drink of water," Deke sneered. "Crowe don't take kindly to strangers mouthing off. Maybe we ought to give you a proper Copper Creek welcome."

Another man chuckled, hand resting on the butt of his revolver.

Cole stopped in the street. His voice stayed low, even, as he said, "Don't start something you ain't ready to finish."

The tension snapped taut. Boots scuffed, spurs chimed faint, and every sound in Copper Creek seemed to die at once. A dog barked once from down an alley, then nothing. Even the wind held its breath.

Deke spat into the dust, a sneer curling his lip. "Looky here, boys. The hero found his tongue." His hand hovered near his pistol, fingers flexing. Two others shifted, eyes hard and narrow, hungry for the chance to draw.

Cole didn't move. His shoulders stayed square, hat brim low, his right hand resting close enough to the Colt on his hip to make every man in sight sweat. His eyes never left Deke. Calm, steady, like a man staring down a rattler.

From the boardwalk, Maggie's voice cut sharp. "Deke Slater, you so much as twitch, and you'll wish you hadn't." She gripped her broom like it was a rifle, Jesse right behind her, fists balled.

The air went tighter still, brittle as glass. Folks peered from windows, whispers scratching. Everyone knew one wrong move here would split the town wide open.

Deke's smile twitched. He wanted to draw—wanted the glory of felling Hardin in the street. But Cole's stillness unnerved him. The man looked carved from stone, like he'd already measured the distance and found Deke lacking.

Cole's voice came again, slow as thunder rolling. "You get one chance. Walk away."

Silence. A bead of sweat traced down Deke's cheek. The other two outlaws shifted, uneasy now, the bravado slipping from their eyes.

Finally, Deke barked a laugh, sharp and ugly. He spat once more and jerked his head toward the saloon. "Ain't worth wastin 'bullets on. Come on, boys."

They moved off, muttering, boots crunching on gravel. The tension bled out of the street in slow, ragged breaths, but it didn't leave clean. Everyone watching knew this wasn't finished.

Cole let his hand ease away from his pistol, though his eyes stayed on their backs until the door swung shut behind them. Only then did he turn, tipping his hat toward Maggie.

"Appreciate the backup," he said.

Maggie snorted, broom still clutched like a weapon. "Next time, Hardin, try not to pick a fight with three men at once."

Cole gave a ghost of a smile. "Didn't pick it. Just didn't walk away."

And deep down, every soul in Copper Creek knew it was only a matter of time before the next spark hit the powder.

* * *

Cole Hardin carried his saddlebags down the quiet street two blocks off Main. Copper Creek was a town that listened with its shutters half-open — the kind of place where whispers traveled faster than horses. Already, heads peeked from doorways as the tall stranger passed.

At the corner stood the boarding house, a broad clapboard structure with lace curtains and a front porch shaded by sagging vines. A faded sign read Rooms for Rent. The paint peeled, but the porch boards had been scrubbed clean that morning.

Cole rapped on the door with the back of his knuckles. It swung open to reveal Widow Martha Hensley — tall, gray-haired, with a spine still straighter than most men in town. She looked him up and down in one sharp sweep.

"You're no drifter," she said. "But you're no townsman either. What are you?"

"Name's Hardin. Just off the trail. Looking for a bed."

Her eyes narrowed, though not without a flicker of curiosity. "You stirred trouble already, didn't you? I saw Crowe's men limping past not half an hour ago. Looked like they'd gone a round with a grizzly."

Cole's mouth tugged into the faintest of smiles. "Wasn't a grizzly."

The widow snorted. "Well, Crowe don't take kindly to being crossed. Renting you a room's as good as painting a target on my door."

Cole reached into his coat and placed two silver dollars on the table inside the hall. "Then call it hazard pay."

The widow studied him for a long moment, then swept the coins up with a nod. "Room's upstairs, second on the left. Dinner's at six, and I don't take lip in my

house. You track dirt on my floors, you'll scrub it yourself.
"

Cole tipped his hat. "Fair enough."

As he climbed the stairs, he passed a thin, nervous-looking man on the landing who wouldn't meet his eyes. From behind one closed door came the sound of muffled coughing. The boarding house wasn't just shelter — it was a collection of drifters, widows, and folk too poor or too proud to leave Copper Creek.

Inside his room, Cole dropped his saddlebags on the floor. The space was plain: an iron bedstead, a washbasin, single window looking out toward the hills. He stood there a moment, hat in his hands, before lowering himself to the chair.

From the street below came the faint echo of boots — hard, heavy, marching in a group. Crowe's men, prowling. The town was holding its breath again.

Cole leaned back in the chair, eyes on the window, jaw set. He wasn't riding out anytime soon.

* * *

The long table in Widow Hensley's dining room smelled of stew, cornbread, and black coffee. The widow ran a tight house — no talking until the blessing, no elbows on the table, and no complaints unless you wanted to cook the next meal yourself.

Cole sat near the end, his broad shoulders taking more space than the chair allowed. Across from him sat a pair of railroad men too poor to leave town and too scared to draw Crowe's notice. Next to them, a gaunt schoolteacher picked at her cornbread.

Widow Hensley herself presided from the head of the table, ladle in hand like a judge's gavel. She kept one eye on Cole through the steam of her stewpot.

"So," she said at last, "the stranger's name is Hardin. Word is you knocked Crowe's men on their backsides in Maggie Caldwell's store. True?"

The room went still. Spoons clinked against bowls and then stopped. Even the coughing upstairs had quieted.

Cole sipped his coffee, unfazed. "They came for trouble. I gave 'em some."

The railroad men shifted nervously. One muttered, "Crowe won't let that pass. He never does."

Widow Hensley's ladle scraped the pot. "Crowe rules by fear. Always has. Sheriff Boone was once a man who might've stood up to him, but…" She let out a humorless laugh. "These days, Silas Boone's just a badge on a bent back. He keeps the peace by looking the other way."

The schoolteacher spoke softly, as if afraid the walls might hear. "Sheriff's not a bad man. Just… worn down. Crowe took his deputy years back. Some wounds never heal."

Cole listened in silence, chewing slowly, eyes fixed on the woodgrain of the table. He filed it all away: Crowe's grip, Boone's fall, the town's broken spirit.

Widow Hensley broke the silence again, voice sharp as vinegar. "You'll need to decide quick, Mr. Hardin. You're either passing through or you're staying. If you stay, you'll bring Crowe's shadow right to this table."

Cole set down his spoon. His voice was steady, even quiet, but it carried through the room like a gunshot. "I'll stay."

The widow studied him for a long moment, then nodded once. "Then eat up. You'll need the strength."

Around the table, the railroad men shifted uncomfortably, the teacher lowered her gaze, but in the far corner, one of the boarders — an old ranch hand with a limp — gave a slow, approving nod.

Outside, boots scuffed on the boardwalk. Crowe's men were making their rounds, loud enough to remind the town they owned the night.

Inside, Cole Hardin finished his stew, his jaw set. The fight was only just beginning.

By the time the sun began to dip, Copper Creek had the feel of a powder keg, waiting for a spark. Dust swirled, whispers stirred, and the whole town seemed to hold its breath. Folks whispered in doorways, Maggie drew her curtains early, and Crowe's men gathered in the saloon like vultures waiting on a carcass.

And Cole Hardin—tall, quiet, calm as a mountain—sat on the porch of the boarding house, rolling himself a smoke and watching.

Everyone in Copper Creek knew it then: the storm had come.

The stranger hadn't left —and Crowe was bound to hear of it.

CHAPTER TWO:
A Town Held Quiet

The fence behind Widow Hensley's boarding house had been leaning for weeks. Cole slipped out before dawn, cup of black coffee in hand. Ever since the last windstorm, the slats stood crooked, held together by prayer and habit more than nails. The old fence stretched straight for twenty feet before pitching sideways like a tired mule. One good kick and it'd fall clean.

Chickens wandered through the gaps every morning to peck around Nate Curry's corral, and every evening someone had to shoo them home.

Cole didn't wait to be asked.

He set his hat on the corner post, rolled up his sleeves, and went to work. The air was clean and quiet, all dew and grass and distant roosters crowing toward daybreak. He uprooted three rotting slats and measured the angles with his eyes alone. Hammered in braces. Shaped a new groove with his pocketknife.

Two of Widow Hensley's grandkids watched from the porch — barefoot, blankets over shoulders, hair all tangled. The little girl whispered first.

"He's fixin 'it."

The boy nodded, thumb still in his mouth. "Without nobody payin 'him."

"You think he likes us?" she whispered.

Cole didn't look up, but there was a smile, hidden behind the hammer blows and early sun.

Widow Hensley found him there twenty minutes later — gloves on, sleeves rolled, shoulder pressed hard against a fencepost while he levered it upright.

"You planning on stealing my property, Mr. Hardin? " she asked from the porch, hands on her hips.

Cole didn't turn. "Only if it falls on me," he said, voice calm under the strain of the post.

The widow snorted. "Should've known. You're the kind of man who thinks being quiet makes him invisible."

He grunted once, righted the post, and wedged a stone to brace it. "You're the kind of woman who sees everything anyway."

Widow Hensley leaned against the porch rail, watching him work. She'd seen men do favors before — the kind that came with strings. But Cole's hands didn't remind her of that kind. He worked like a man who was used to being alone, not one who was aching to impress.

"You ever build a house, Hardin?" she asked.

"No," he said, pulling a hammer from his belt. "Built enough fences and lean-tos to know the shape of the land, though."

"You married?"

"No."

She nodded. "That explains not being afraid of splinters."

That got a ghost of a smile from him — the kind that arrived slow, like a stranger testing a doorway before stepping inside.

Cole wiped sweat from his brow, having straightened nearly six fence slats.

"You want breakfast?" she asked, voice steady but warm.

Cole hesitated. "Didn't mean to trouble you."

"You trouble folks by leavin 'things worse than you found them," she said. "You do the opposite. The least I can do is put a biscuit on a plate."

Cole finally nodded. "Biscuits sound mighty fine."

Widow Hensley disappeared into her kitchen, muttering about bacon, while the children crept barefoot into the yard — first just to peek, then to bring him the extra nails from the coffee can beside the steps.

When Maggie Caldwell passed by later on her way to the store, she paused mid-step. She took in the scene — Cole working in the dirt, children handing him tools, fence straighter than it'd been in years.

She leaned on her broom. "You're a hard man to read, Hardin," she called.

Cole glanced over, thumb still pressing splinters flat. "Only cause folks keep tryin'."

Maggie huffed. "Alright, fine. You're a good man doin 'things without bein 'asked. Better?"

"Doesn't matter if it's better," Cole said, stepping back from the repaired fence. "Matters if it holds."

Maggie watched him for a long moment. Something in her sharpness dulled, just a touch — not soft, but real.

"Good fences keep folks safe," she said.

Cole nodded. "And bad ones make it easy for wolves to walk through."

Maggie's eyes narrowed at that — not at him, but at the truth hidden inside it.

A few minutes later, Jesse wandered over from the street, dragging a bucket of feed. He stopped when he saw Cole pounding nails into the uprights.

"You fixin 'her fence?" Jesse asked, eyes bright with something like admiration.

Cole wiped sweat from his brow. "Figure the chickens've earned a little dignity."

26

Jesse laughed — loud and sudden, like it surprised him. He grabbed a spare nail pouch off the ground. "Can I help?"

Cole handed him the hammer. "Only if you don't hit your thumb."

Jesse grinned. "I got ten thumbs. One's bound to survive."

Widow Hensley shook her head — but her smile was real this time.

Behind them, the town went on like usual: smoke rose from the smithy, Maggie swept her porch, and Tom's hammer clanged against metal at the forge. But something subtle had started to shift.

People passing by slowed down. Watched. Not out of curiosity — but out of recognition.

Because nothing said a man belonged like seeing him mend something he didn't break.

By the time Cole picked up his hat and headed in for breakfast, the kids waved from the porch — shy the first time, then bold.

He raised a hand in return.

Not out of politeness.

Out of something almost like belonging.

And in that stretch of morning sun, with fence slats straightening and nails thudding home, Cole Hardin's roots in Copper Creek sank just a hair deeper.

* * *

Inside the livery, the smell of hay and horse sweat hung thick, and the only sounds were the shuffle of hooves and the rasp of a brush across a flank.

Cole worked in silence, sleeves rolled up, shirt damp with the kind of honest sweat that comes from labor, not running. He moved easy among the stalls, unhurried but efficient. The horses read that calm; they shifted their weight, snorted, and let him near.

Old Nate Curry leaned against the doorway, gray whiskers bristling around the stem of his pipe. "You handle horses like a man who's been broke once or twice himself," he said, smoke curling lazily into the chill air.

Cole's mouth curved faintly as he cinched the strap on a saddle. "Difference is, I learned."

Nate barked a short laugh. "Reckon that's more than most men manage." He shuffled over, boots scuffing. "Most of the fellas around here take more breakin 'than the stock."

Cole grunted, testing the cinch with a tug. "I've noticed."

Outside, a wagon rattled by — Tom, the blacksmith, heading toward his forge, nodding once through the open doors. "Hardin," he said in greeting, voice rough from years of smoke and hammer. Cole returned the nod, nothing more, and Tom tipped his hat before moving on.

A few minutes later, the Penrose girl came in for feed — Clara, all wide eyes and windblown hair, her father's team hitched outside. "Morning, Nate," she said, setting a coin on the counter. "Pa says you still owe him a favor for that mule trade."

Nate waved a hand. "Tell your pa the mule's still got both ears and a bad attitude. We're even."

She grinned, then glanced toward Cole. "Don't think I've seen you before."

"New in town," Cole said, not looking up from the saddle he was checking.

"Don't mind him," Nate said. "He's the quiet kind. Means he's either dangerous or smart. Time'll tell which."

Clara laughed softly, collected her feed, and left. Cole straightened, catching Nate's grin.

"You enjoy stirrin 'up talk, don't you?"

"Only thing keeps the dust from settlin 'too thick." Nate thumped his pipe against a post. "You got the touch

29

with horses, Hardin. Folks'll pay to have you around if you stick. Copper Creek doesn't trust strangers easy, but they come around when a man works."

Cole nodded, wiping sweat from his brow. "Work's honest. It'll do."

For a moment, the two men stood in quiet, listening to the wind hum against the loose boards. It was the same wind that had blown across every frontier town since the world began — dry, persistent, whispering of distance and change.

"You plan on stayin 'long?" Nate asked finally.

Cole looked out toward the rising sun. The streets were still empty, only a few silhouettes moving by the well. "Depends," he said. "On the sort of men runnin ' things."

Nate's grin faded. "Ah. Then you'll be wantin 'to meet Crowe."

"Not in any hurry to."

"Wise." Nate spat into the dirt. "Crowe doesn't like men he can't buy or scare."

Cole tugged the saddle girth once more, then set his hand flat on the horse's neck. "Then I guess we'll see which I am."

* * *

Morning came slow in Copper Creek. The dust rose with the sun, and by the time Cole Hardin stepped out into the street, the air shimmered with heat. He tugged his hat lower and set out down Main Street.

Everywhere he went, eyes followed. A drifter in most towns might draw curiosity — here, he drew fear. Mothers pulled children inside, shopkeepers closed shutters with sudden purpose. Folks weren't unfriendly. They were cautious. Like everything they owned might be taken if they so much as smiled at the wrong man.

Cole started with the blacksmith, old Tom Harper. Sparks flew from the forge, but Tom paused, wiping soot from his brow as the tall stranger approached.

"You the one tangled with Crowe's boys?" Tom asked, voice low.

Cole only nodded.

"Careful. Man, like Crowe don't forget a bruisin'. Still..." Tom hesitated, then thrust out a rough, soot-streaked hand. "Town could use more men that don't spook easy."

From there, Cole wandered. At the telegraph office, the operator barely looked up, muttering about "wires down again" — but Cole saw the man's hands tremble. At the barber's shop, a half-shaved farmer whispered that Crowe had doubled his "protection fee." Even the saloon, where a piano sat gathering dust, held only silence.

Three of Crowe's men at the bar stared at Cole with predator eyes.

By afternoon, Cole found himself back at Caldwell's store. Jesse was sweeping the porch with more enthusiasm than skill, darting glances down the street like a boy itching for trouble. Maggie leaned in the doorway, arms crossed.

"You're still here," she said. "Crowe's not gonna like that."

"Never figured to live my life making Crowe comfortable," Cole replied.

Jesse grinned. "Wish more folks thought like that."

Maggie shot the boy a look. "Don't you go encouraging him. This town's got enough trouble." But her tone carried a flicker of respect she hadn't shown before.

Sheriff Silas Boone appeared not long after, trudging down the street with shoulders bent. He stopped when he saw Cole, badge dull in the sunlight. "Hardin," Boone said. "Best advice I'll give you: ride out while you can. Ain't no shame in leaving a fight you can't win."

Cole's eyes narrowed. "You saying you never tried?"

Boone's face tightened, jaw working. He said nothing more, just tipped his hat and moved on. He'd once been the lawman who'd been something more than a shadow.

By evening, Cole sat on the boarding house porch, watching the sun sink behind the hills. The town lay quiet, as though waiting for a storm. Widow Hensley brought him a cup of coffee, her voice low.

"Crowe will move soon. He always does when he's been made a fool."

Cole nodded, sipping slow. "Then I'll be ready."

Across the street, a rider sat his horse too long in the twilight, watching. When Cole's eyes met his, the rider turned and disappeared into the growing dark.

The hammer hadn't fallen yet. But Copper Creek could feel it coming.

* * *

The riders came back empty-handed.

Their horses were lathered and wild-eyed from the run, dust still clinging to the sweat on their flanks. The men who dismounted didn't look much better — bruised, grazed, breathing too hard. One had a torn sleeve soaked through with blood. Another cradled his bandaged wrist like it might fall off if he let go. They were all covered with molasses.

They gathered in the clearing behind Crowe's camp, trying to look casual, trying not to show the way their hands shook. It didn't work.

Crowe sat on a split log in the center of the circle, long legs stretched out, a lit cigar painting his face in low amber. Its glow flickered in his eyes — cold, fixed, the color of a rattlesnake's patience right before the strike.

Deke stepped forward to speak first, hat in hand. "So… Hardin—"

Crowe didn't look up. "Hardin's still walkin 'free?" he said, the words flat as dead air.

Deke swallowed. "Well, he—"

"He *what*?" Crowe asked calmly, lifting his gaze at last.

A terrible silence spread through the clearing. The men shifted, all trying not to draw attention.

Calhoun finally spoke up, voice spiraling into a nervous wheeze. "He fought back. Tore into us like a wildcat. Would've finished me if—"

Crowe stood. The cigar dropped from his fingers. He crushed it under his heel on the dirt.

"You let one man — *one man* — walk in here, spit in my hand, and walk out again in one piece?"

"He—I mean—" Calhoun backed a step.

34

Crowe drew his pistol and aimed it at the man's foot. The shot cracked like thunder. Calhoun screamed and fell, clutching his boot as the others stiffened in place.

Crowe didn't flinch. He holstered the gun slow. Looked around the circle.

"You boys forget who I am?" he asked, voice quiet and razor-sharp. "Forget how this works? Copper Creek pays because it fears me. They stay quiet because they know I make examples. You take that away from me, and what am I?"

A cold breeze cut through the trees. No one answered.

Crowe leaned closer, teeth bared in something that wasn't quite a smile." I'm the man who built this empire with blood and fire. And now some broken-down saddle tramp thinks he can walk through my town like he owns it?"

He straightened, eyes gone flat and deadly. "That don't stand. Not for a day. Not for an hour."

He turned to Deke. "Next time you see Hardin, you don't come back unless you've got him tied across your saddle or dead in the dust. You hear me?"

Deke nodded, but Crowe grabbed him by the shirt front and yanked him close. "No. Say it."

Deke choked. "I hear you, Crowe. Loud and clear."

Crowe shoved him backward, wiping his palm on his coat like the touch pained him. "Good. Because Copper Creek needs remindin', I'll give 'em a reminder they won't forget."

He swept his gaze across the camp, let the silence settle like a loaded gun. "You boys get ready. We're goin ' back. Not to collect taxes. Not for questions. This time, we go to make 'em bleed."

The men stiffened, fear tightening their guts. Because they knew what was coming next. Everyone did.

Cole Hardin had drawn a line the day he came to town.

Now Crowe was about to make sure the whole world knew what happened to anyone who crossed it.

* * *

The sun had barely slipped behind the ridge line when the first flames rose.

Patrick Clancy woke to the acrid sting of smoke in his nostrils. At first, he thought it was the wood stove smoking, but then came the frantic pounding of hooves in the corral and the unmistakable roar of fire. He stumbled out of bed, pulling on his boots, his bad leg protesting as he lurched toward the window. What he saw stole his breath—his barn, his livelihood, lit up like judgment day.

"Dear God," he whispered, fumbling for his suspenders as he hobbled outside. The night sky glowed red, and sparks rained down like fiery snow. Inside the barn, his horses screamed, wild with terror, the sound tearing through the valley like a knife.

Cole smelled the smoke before he heard the shouts. Someone was banging on his door.

"Hardin! Crowe's men— they lit up Clancy's barn!"

Cole was already moving, buckling his gunbelt as he strode into the night. The sky to the east glowed red, and the crackle of fire carried on the wind. Horses screamed from the barn, and voices shouted in panic.

By the time he reached the blaze, half the town was gathered, faces pale in the firelight. Men hauled buckets from the well, women herded frightened children back, but the barn was already lost—roaring like a furnace.   Neighbors were running across the fields with buckets and shovels, drawn by the glow.

And painted on the barn door, black against the flames, was Crowe's calling card: a crude "C" scorched into the wood with hot iron.

Cole's jaw tightened.

Maggie Caldwell had Jesse by the hand, the boy's eyes wide in shock. "Pat!" she cried, "Your barn—!"

"I can see it!" Clancy barked, though fear cracked his voice. He limped toward the double doors, heat slapping his face as smoke billowed out. He grabbed for the iron latch, burning his palms, and cursed loud enough for the Devil himself to hear.

Then a voice, calm but firm, cut through the chaos. "Stand back."

Cole Hardin strode out of the darkness, long coat trailing, eyes steady. He ripped off his duster, wrapped it around his arm, and kicked the barn doors wide. The inferno's breath poured out, but Cole didn't flinch. He disappeared into the smoke.

"Is he mad?" Clancy croaked, shielding his eyes as flames licked higher.

Moments later, a terrified chestnut mare burst from the haze, Cole at her flank, guiding her to safety. He smacked her hindquarters, sending her bolting toward the corral, then vanished back into the smoke. One by one, he brought the animals out—two geldings, a stubborn mule, even Clancy's prized bay stallion, coughing and half-wild with fear.

The townsfolk formed a line, passing buckets, shouting orders, but it was clear the barn itself was lost. The dry timbers popped and groaned like gunfire, beams sagging inward. The fire roared its victory to the stars.

Clancy stood there, helpless, tears cutting trails through the soot on his cheeks. A year's worth of feed. His tack. Tools he'd carried since he was a boy in Ireland. All gone. He clutched at his limp leg as if it might give way.
"Everything I built…" he whispered.

Cole staggered out one final time, his face blackened with ash, carrying a foal in his arms. He laid the trembling creature at Clancy's feet and straightened, chest heaving, eyes narrowing past the firelight.

On the ridge above the ranch, silhouetted against the flames, sat horsemen. Six of them. Their laughter carried on the night wind. At their center, tall in the saddle, was a figure with a wide black hat—Jed Crowe.

Crowe's voice rolled across the valley like thunder. "This is what happens when folks forget who runs Copper Creek!"

Then he wheeled his horse and rode off into the night, his men trailing like shadows.

The crowd murmured in fear. Some spat curses, others hung their heads. But all eyes turned at last to Cole Hardin, standing against the glow of ruin, his shoulders square, his face hard as cut stone.

Clancy swallowed the lump in his throat and croaked out the only words he could find. "Thank you, mister."

Cole's gaze stayed fixed on the ridgeline where Crowe had been, his voice low, steady. "Don't thank me yet, Pat. This was just the start."

The fire crackled behind him, lighting his silhouette like a figure carved from iron. And for the first time that night, the townsfolk felt a stir of something they'd near forgotten—hope, sharp and dangerous as a drawn blade.

Maggie clutched Jesse to her side, her eyes hard. Around them, the townsfolk looked from the fire to Cole— waiting to see if this tall stranger would stand or ride out.

Cole turned slowly, scanning the gathered faces, then spoke low but firm, his voice cutting through the crackle of fire. "Crowe wanted to send a message. Well, he's gonna find out I got one to send back."

CHAPTER THREE:
Showdown at Dawn

Copper Creek woke to fresh scars. The night fire had gutted Patrick Clancy's barn. By dawn, the smell of scorched hay and charred wood hung heavy in Copper Creek. The rancher himself stood in the ashes, hat in his hands, his limp more pronounced as he tried to beat back the smoke with a rake. His cattle lowed restlessly in the corral, spooked by the smell of ruin.

Red paint — thick, dripping — slashed across the front of Caldwell's General & Dry Goods like blood smeared by a giant's hand. One word, big enough to read from the far end of Main Street:

PAY.

Below it, smaller: Or Burn.

It was Crowe's handwriting. The whole town knew it.

The sheriff lingered on the boardwalk, hat in his hands, too weary to raise his voice, eyes fixed on the ground.

The morning sun struck Copper Creek hard, glinting off the saloon windows and washing the street in a pale, unforgiving light. Smoke still hung faint from the Clancy's place where Crowe's men had ridden roughshod the night before. Folks went about their business quiet, eyes down, the fear from the fire still raw.

Then the batwing doors of the Silver Star Saloon banged open. Jed Crowe stepped out, flanked by Deke

Slater and two more of his men. His black hat sat low, his silver revolver gleaming in the sun. He looked down the street with the lazy arrogance of a man convinced the town was his.

"Copper Creek!" he shouted, voice cutting through the still air. "Seems we got ourselves a stranger don't know the rules. Let me remind all of you who runs this town."

People froze. A woman carrying laundry ducked into a doorway. The blacksmith lowered his hammer with a shaky hand.

From the crowd, a voice cracked the stillness: "Why Clancy?"

Crowe leaned forward with a grin that didn't reach his eyes.

"Well now," he drawled, smoke curling from the cigar clenched between his teeth. "That's a good question. You want an answer? Here it is."

He swept his gaze across the gathered faces — Maggie's tight jaw, Jesse's clenched fists, Widow Hensley's grim stare. Then he locked eyes with Cole Hardin, standing calm but unflinching in the dust.

Crowe's grin was sharp as a knife. "A man who stands against me, stands against Copper Creek. And that's a mistake no one makes twice."

He looked around, waiting for someone to answer, daring them to.

The crowd parted as a tall figure came down the boardwalk, slow and steady. Cole Hardin. His shadow stretched long in the dust, his stride unhurried, his shoulders squared. He stopped in the center of the street, the distance between him and Crowe measured in heartbeats.

"You talk loud in the morning, Crowe," Cole said, his voice calm, steady as bedrock. "But I reckon folks here already know who you are. They don't need reminding."

A ripple went through the crowd—half shock, half relief.

Crowe's eyes narrowed. "You got a mouth on you, Hardin. Careful, it don't get you killed."

Deke Slater stepped forward, hand hovering near his pistol. "Let me handle him, boss. One shot, he won't—"

"Hold," Crowe snapped, though his hand rested easy on his own gun. His grin returned, thin and cold. "No. This one's mine."

The street was silent but for the creak of a shutter in the wind.

Sheriff Boone finally stepped out, sweat glistening on his brow. "Jed, for God's sake, not here, not now…"

Crowe ignored him. His eyes locked on Cole. "You want to play hero, Hardin? Then you better be ready to bleed for it."

Cole didn't flinch. He shifted his weight, boots planted firm in the dust. "I've bled before. Question is— are you ready to lose what you think you own?"

The words hung heavy, and for the first time in years, the people of Copper Creek saw Jed Crowe blink.

A storm was brewing, and every soul in town knew it.

"As long as Cole Hardin stands up to me," Crowe said, voice carrying like a whipcrack, "you won't know where I'll strike next. Could be your barn. Could be your herd. Could be the roof over your children's heads. That's the cost of one man's pride."

Gasps rippled through the crowd. Mothers pulled their children close. Clancy sagged against the corral fence, his ruin plain for all to see.

Crowe smiled wider, cruel as the sun on steel. "So you tell me, Copper Creek — how long you gonna let Hardin bring my wrath down on your heads?"

His men laughed, horses shifting restlessly. Fear spread through the onlookers like a sickness. Some eyes turned toward Cole — wary, doubtful.

But Cole didn't flinch. He met Crowe's gaze steady as stone, jaw tight, eyes burning.

. No one answered. Only the creak of signs in the morning breeze.

The corner of Crowe's mouth twitched. "And you, Hardin. Thought you'd play the hero, didn't ya? Humiliatin my boys in front of the whole town."

Cole didn't move, didn't blink. "Didn't see any heroes from your side last night. Just men starting' a barn fire and too yellow to fight it."

A ripple of nervous gasps ran through the townsfolk. Crowe's face darkened, his jaw working. One of his men shifted in the saddle, hand drifting toward his revolver, but Crowe held him back with a glance.

"You got guts, Hardin. I'll give you that. But guts don't mean nothin 'when you're standin 'alone. This town knows better. Ain't that right, folks?"

He looked around, daring anyone to speak. No one did. They lowered their eyes, ashamed.

Cole moved slow, deliberate, his boots crunching in the dust, every eye on him. He stopped, facing Crowe square. "Maybe they ain't ready to stand yet. But I am. And the way I see it, Copper Creek don't belong to you. Not today, not tomorrow, not ever."

The silence stretched thin as a whipcord. Crows cawed from the rooftops. Crowe's men shifted in their saddles, itching for blood.

Crowe leaned back in his saddle, grinning like a wolf. "Then it's you and me, Hardin. And I aim to bury you before this town starts gettin 'ideas."

He spat in the dust, and, with a jerk of his reins, wheeled his horse. "Enjoy your day, Hardin. It might be your last."

The gang thundered off, hooves shaking the ground. The townsfolk stirred, murmuring in fearful tones. All eyes turned to Cole—standing alone in the middle of the street, watching Crowe ride out with the same calm resolve he'd carried into the barn fire.

Maggie's voice broke the hush, sharp as a rifle crack. "Well, what are you all starin 'at? Man's right—we don't stand now, we never will."

Jesse puffed up beside her, broom in his hands like a saber. Some folks nodded, others looked away. But for the first time, the seed of defiance had taken root.

Cole tipped his hat low, eyes still fixed on the horizon where Crowe had gone. "This ain't finished. Not by a long mile."

And for the first time, Copper Creek realized the fight wasn't just between two men. It was for the soul of the town.

* * *

The dust had barely settled when Cole crossed the street. The townsfolk drifted back to their shops and porches, muttering under their breath, but their eyes never strayed far from him. He moved easy, boots crunching in the dirt, as though he hadn't just been singled out by the most dangerous man in Copper Creek.

The smell of coffee and frying bacon greeted him as he pushed through the door of Miss Lila's Restaurant, the only place in town where you could get a plate of eggs without grit in your teeth. The bell above the door jingled. Conversation hushed.

Lila herself stood behind the counter, a stout woman in her forties with arms strong from years of rolling dough. She fixed Cole with a wary look, then slid a steaming mug of coffee onto the counter. "Figured you'd be in sooner or later. Town's been talkin'."

Cole settled onto a stool, resting his hat on the counter. He wrapped his hands around the mug, savoring the warmth. "Talkin 'good or bad?"

She shrugged, pouring coffee for another customer." Depends who's doin 'the talkin'. Some say you're a fool for pokin 'Crowe. Others say maybe you're the kind of fool we need."

A nervous laugh rippled from a corner table. Two ranch hands bent over their plates, whispering. A pair of Crowe's men slouched by the window, nursing beers though it wasn't even noon. They watched Cole like hawks, hands never straying far from their belts.

Cole cut into his eggs with the edge of his fork, slow and steady. "Only thing I poked was their pride. They'll get over it."

The men by the window snorted, one of them muttering something ugly under his breath. Lila shot them a sharp look. "You two wanna eat, you eat. Otherwise get out."

They grinned and stayed put, their eyes hard on Cole.

"Where are you stayin?" Lila asked Cole.

"Widow Hensley's boarding house," he said.

The door banged open and Maggie Caldwell swept in, Jesse trailing after her. She marched straight to the counter, broom still in hand like she'd been born with it. "If you're gonna sit there fillin 'your belly, mister, you best know Jed Crowe don't let things lie. He'll come back, and next time it won't be a barn."

Cole set down his fork and looked her square in the eye, calm as the morning sun. "Then I'll be sittin 'right here when he does."

The room went quiet again, the words hanging like gun smoke. The townsfolk exchanged nervous glances, but a few of them—just a few—looked at Cole with something more than fear in their eyes. Something closer to hope.

* * *

Maggie stood in front of her store, hands fisted at her sides, jaw locked hard enough to crack a molar. A bucket of water rested on the boardwalk beside her, bristling with brushes. She stared at the letters a long moment — the threat, the insult, the false promise of ownership — before dipping a rag and scrubbing in hard, furious strokes.

The paint didn't give easy. It bled in long streaks down the siding, soaking her sleeves, staining her skin. She didn't stop. Didn't look around. Didn't even wipe the sweat from her brow.

If he wanted to shame her, he'd have to try harder.

Across the street, Cole Hardin stood under the awning outside Lila's, coffee mug in hand. His hat tipped low, shadowing his eyes. But he was watching.

Not just Maggie. The *town.*

Faces peeked from curtained windows. Boots lingered at door thresholds. No one helped her. No one stopped her.

Jesse burst out of the store with another bucket and splashed it down.

"Mama, let me—"

"No," Maggie snapped, rag working like a saw. "He wants us to look afraid. I ain't obliging him."

Jesse's cheeks reddened. Not from shame — from fury that had nowhere to go.

49

Cole crossed the street. "You need a hand?" he asked.

Maggie didn't pause. "I need a lot of things, Hardin. A fresh coat of paint. A sheriff who ain't afraid. Half a town with a spine."

Her words cut, but they weren't aimed at him.

Cole nodded, quiet. "I'll get the ladder." He turned, but Jesse caught his arm.

"You gonna stand with us or not?" the boy asked, voice low, eyes burning.

Cole paused. "I ain't here to play hero."

"Too late," Jesse said. "Everybody saw you help at the barn fire. That's all it takes. Now you're part of it."

Cole met his gaze. Jesse didn't flinch. "You're young," Cole said. "Don't ever mistake one good deed for a war."

"Ain't that what a war's made of?" Jesse shot back. "Small choices until someone's got to choose loud."

Cole exhaled slow. Looked up at the word on the wall, half-washed now, bleeding red onto the boards.

"I don't run from trouble," he said at last. "But I don't invite it, neither."

50

Jesse stared at him. "Trouble already invited you."

Maggie stepped back from the wall then, breathing hard. She turned to Cole without asking him again — just looked, just waited.

Cole didn't blink. "All right," he said. "Let's get the rest of it off."

For the next hour, Cole worked beside her, shirt sleeves rolled, shoulders bent, scrubbing the last vestiges of Crowe's threat from the boards. Jesse carried water, refilled brushes, never once letting go of that rifle hanging at his back.

People watched. They pretended not to. But they watched.

And when the last of the paint came off, Maggie straightened, wet rag dripping, chest rising and falling with hard-earned breath. She looked at the clean wood. Not perfect. But not claimed.

"Thank you," she told Cole — not soft. Just true.

Cole nodded once. "Man's got to know what he's standin 'behind."

"And what's that?" Jesse asked.

"Decency," Cole said.

He didn't look at the paint. Didn't look at the windows full of silent eyes.

He looked out at Copper Creek — and saw the smallest shift.

A few men stepped fully onto the sidewalk instead of hiding. A mother let her boy walk closer. Holt closed his Bible and nodded once from his steps. Nate Curry tipped his hat from the edge of the street.

A town's courage didn't roar that day.

But it shifted.

Because Cole Hardin hadn't said he was fighting.

He'd just stopped pretending he wasn't.

* * *

The saloon was half-lit, half-loud, and fully alive by the time Cole pushed through the swinging doors that night. A haze of pipe smoke hovered up near the rafters, curling like ghosts around the oil lamps. Piano keys stumbled through a tune someone barely remembered, and the smell of whiskey and leather tangled in the air.

No one stopped and stared like they used to when strangers walked in.

Three men nodded from across the room.

That was something.

Cole made for the counter first. The barkeep — a broad man named Amos King — nodded once and reached for a bottle without being asked.

"Hard day?" he asked, sliding the glass across.

"Good enough to earn the drink," Cole said, lifting it.

Amos grinned. "And bad enough to need it."

Cole didn't answer. Just drank and let the pause carry the joke where it needed to go.

To his right, a card table scraped a chair back. Three farmers and one ranch hand looked up.

"You in, Hardin?" the ranch hand asked. "Seat's open. So's the luck."

Cole tapped the bar twice, then walked over, boots easy on the scuffed boards. He sat, cards dealt, and folded the first hand without blinking.

"You always play that careful," one of the farmers said, smirking.

Cole shrugged. "Only when I'm tired of losing."

Laughter lifted around the table, the kind that pulled everyone within earshot closer — including Reverend Holt, who stood just inside the doorway, coat still buttoned, hat low, eyes the kind that took everything in.

He didn't sit. Not yet. Just watched. Listening.

Talk at the table drifted — weather, calves hitting early, a busted wagon wheel, Widow Hensley's biscuits, which were widely agreed to be the best a man could get without offering marriage.

Then it shifted.

As it always did after a few drinks.

"Crowe's boys passed through again this morning," the ranch hand said, lowering his cards just a fraction.

"Didn't stop," said another. "Didn't say a word."

"No," Amos called from the counter. "Didn't need to."

The chatter died. The piano quieted. Even the deck of cards felt heavier in Cole's hands.

One of the farmers, older, grayer, jaw set like stone, leaned forward and said the words that had been sitting in everyone's throat:

"What happens when he pushes again? When he starts taking men like he took barns? What're we supposed to do then?"

Reverend Holt stepped out of the doorway then — not in to preach, not in to stir, just close enough so he could be heard.

"That's the question, isn't it?"

Eyes flicked toward him — and then toward Cole.

He held his cards loosely, thumb at the edge, gaze steady on the man who'd asked.

Cole put his hand down on the table. Slowly. Deliberately.

"When a man's had enough," he said, voice low but clear, "you'll know it."

The room didn't stir for three full heartbeats.

Not a sip. Not a step.

That wasn't boasting. Wasn't a threat. Wasn't even loud.

It was a line drawn.

Then Amos let out a slow breath. Someone shuffled their cards. The piano started up again. But every man and woman in that room walked out later knowing three things:

Cole Hardin wasn't leaving.
Cole Hardin wasn't scared.
And sooner or later, Copper Creek was going to have to make the same choice.

* * *

The lantern on Maggie Caldwell's porch still burned when Cole walked back from the saloon. Crickets sang up from the creekbeds. Most of the town lay dark and closed — but light still glowed behind the curtains of the general store.

Jesse was waiting, sitting cross-legged on the porch step with a broom across his knees. He stood as soon as Cole came into view.

"You meant it — what you said in there."

Cole paused, eyes narrowing just a little. "You were at the saloon?"

"No," Jesse said, stepping forward. "But I heard. Amos came by for supplies. Said you told everyone you'd had enough."

Cole let the silence stand.

Something in Jesse trembled — not fear, but urgency. The need for someone bigger, stronger, braver to anchor what he already believed.

"Folks are lookin 'to you," Jesse said. "They were afraid before. But now they're angry. We know we can't take Crowe alone, but if you—"

Cole cut in — not sharp, but firm. "I'm not here to play hero, Jesse."

Jesse swallowed and stepped down off the porch, two feet from Cole now. The boy's hands curled into fists at his sides.

"You've already got a target on your back," Jesse said. "You know that. But you walk around actin 'like it don't matter. You help people. Fix fences. Sit at saloons without backing down. You say it ain't about being a hero — but everybody sees it. Everybody knows what you're doing."

Cole looked away toward the dark street — toward the quiet houses and shuttered windows.

And Jesse, finding courage he didn't know he had, said something that hit home harder than a gunstock:

"You don't get to do all that and then say it's not your fight."

Cole stood still, jaw clenching once. "I didn't come to lead a rebellion," he said, voice low.

"No," Jesse said. "But you make people start thinkin 'they might win one."

Silence.

Not defeat. Not tension. Just truth laid bare between them — one young and desperate, the other tired of carrying a life defined by leaving before the smoke cleared.

And for the first time, Cole didn't correct him.

He just looked at Jesse — really looked at him — and shook his head slow.

"You got more guts than some men twice your age, " Cole muttered.

Jesse lifted his chin. "Maybe I learned it watchin ' you."

Something inside Cole tightened — not pain, not regret. A weight he hadn't asked for. But one he wasn't sure he could shed anymore.

He looked out again toward the dark horizon, where Crowe and all that ugliness waited.

"When the time comes," he said at last, "I won't step aside."

Jesse let out a slow breath — shaky, but full of fire.

"That's all we needed to hear."

Behind them, the lantern flickered. And all up and down Copper Creek, windows closed just a little less tight.

Because whether he wanted the mantle or not, Cole Hardin had just crossed the line between "passing through" and "standing for."

CHAPTER FOUR:
Breakfast, Ashes and Resolve

By the time Cole crossed the street, the sun had cleared the rooftops, setting the dust to glitter. Copper Creek was waking — boots on boardwalks, wagon wheels creaking, a dog nosing through the trash behind the saloon.

Maggie's General Store was already open, its porch swept clean, barrels of flour and seed stacked neat by the door. The hand-painted sign above the window read Caldwell's General Store, and Maggie ran the place herself with Jesse at her side.

The smell hit him as soon as he stepped inside — coffee, bacon grease, a trace of oil from the rifles hanging on the back wall. Shelves lined with everything a town needed to keep breathing: nails, sugar, lamp wicks, chewing tobacco.

"About time you showed your face," Maggie said from behind the counter, hands on her hips. "You can't live on jerky and black coffee forever."

Cole tipped his hat. "Wasn't planning on dyin 'on it, either."

"Sit," she said, already reaching for a plate. "You're eatin 'proper today."

Before he could argue, she slid a stool out with her boot. Jesse appeared from the back room carrying a skillet, eyes bright despite the early hour. "Made too much anyway," the boy said, setting it down. "Figured you might come by."

Maggie snorted. "Figured right. The man looks half-starved."

Cole sat, more out of politeness than hunger, and Jesse filled his plate — eggs, biscuits, and bacon that gleamed with just the right amount of grease. Maggie poured him coffee so black it looked like it might bite back.

The store was already stirring with life. Two ranchers stood by the barrels of feed, arguing in low voices about a missing steer. The old widow Hensley was buying thread, tsking about the preacher's new sermon being "too soft by half."

Maggie clucked her tongue. "Reverend Holt's got his hands full. Crowe's men took half the offering plate last Sunday, said it was 'protection dues.'"

Jesse looked up from where he was cleaning the counter. "Protection from what?"

Maggie's rag froze. "That's the question, ain't it?"

Cole sipped his coffee, eyes half-lidded. "A man can only pay tribute so long before he calls it theft."

The words cut through the chatter like a nail through pine. Every head turned his way — not hostile, but wary. Words like that carried weight in Copper Creek, the kind that could draw attention from the wrong men.

Eben, leaning in the doorway with his hat in hand, gave a slow nod. "Ain't heard anyone say it plain in a while," he said.

Maggie shot Cole a sharp look, part warning, part approval. "Careful how loud you talk, Hardin. Walls have ears in this town, and most of 'em report to Crowe."

Cole met her gaze over the rim of his cup. "Then maybe it's time someone stopped whisperin'."

The room went still again, and for a long moment the only sound was the ticking of the clock behind the counter. Then Widow Hensley cleared her throat and said, "Well. I for one think the man's right."

Maggie's mouth twitched. "Don't start a revolution in my store before breakfast."

A ripple of laughter broke the tension, small but real. People relaxed a little, resumed their talk — though the air felt different now, charged.

Cole finished his coffee, dropped a few coins on the counter. "Good meal," he said.

Maggie waved a hand. "Come back when you want another. Lord knows I can't eat all Jesse cooks."

He nodded once, tugged his hat down, and stepped back into the sunlight. Behind him, the store filled with the low hum of voices again — softer now, but carrying a new thread through them.

Not hope exactly. Not yet.
But maybe the start of it.

* * *

The air still smelled of smoke.

Gray curls drifted over the blackened skeleton of Clancy's barn, what had once been half-timbered walls now reduced to jagged beams and mounds of ash. The grass around the foundation was scorched and dead. Burned boards sagged inward like ribs in a body too tired to keep standing.

Clancy stood alone in the rubble, hands shaking at his sides. The old Irishman wasn't crying, but his face looked like someone had taken more than lumber from him. Like years and dignity had burned right along with it.

Cole came up the rise on foot, coat off, his sleeves rolled above the elbow. He didn't call out. Just stopped at the fence line for a moment, taking it all in.

Clancy heard footsteps and turned, blinking through the wind.

"Hardin," he said, voice raw. "Come to watch me bury what's left of my work?"

Cole said nothing. He just stepped over the fence, picked up a broken beam the length of his arm, and tossed it aside like he was sorting lumber, not loss.

Clancy frowned. "You don't have to—"

62

Cole walked past him, calm but deliberate, grabbed a bent pitchfork from the dirt, and began turning through the ashes — not carefully, but methodically. Searching for ground worth rebuilding on.

"We'll need a rake," Cole said, like he was talking about a fence board instead of someone's memories. "And a spade. And whatever's left that ain't burned through."

Clancy stared. "You… planning to rebuild it?"

Cole paused just long enough to meet his gaze. "You planning to quit on it?"

The older man let out a sound — half-scoff, half-laugh. Then he shoved his hands on his hips and nodded.

"Ain't never quit a day in my life," he muttered. "Not even when my first wife left me for a telegraph operator."

Cole raised an eyebrow. "That a true story?"

"Sure as the marriage was short," Clancy said.

They worked in silence awhile. Cole cleared the wreckage, stacked what could be saved, and raked the ash from the foundation to see what could be used. Every movement was steady, measured — not like a hired hand, but like a man who already understood the value of sweat and structure.

"Why're you really here, Hardin?" Clancy asked, leaning on the bent gate.

Cole looked out over the burned field, the blackened earth. The barn that wasn't. The brand of fear stamped across every scorched board.

"Because Crowe wants you small," Cole said. "And this is the day you decide if you stay that way."

Clancy kicked a pile of ash and sniffed. "Feels like the town already decided."

"Not all of 'em," Cole said.

Clancy studied the stranger who wasn't really a stranger anymore. The muscles in his jaw worked once, twice.

"You ain't afraid of him?"

Cole kept raking. "I'm tired of men like Crowe running things."

Clancy nodded slowly. "Hell," he said. "Maybe this town needed someone like you before it burned."

"Maybe it did," Cole said. "But burnin 'ain't the end." He threw another blackened board onto a pile. "It's where you start again."

* * *

The saloon was half-lit, half-loud, and fully alive by the time Cole pushed through the swinging doors that night. A haze of pipe smoke hovered up near the rafters, curling like ghosts around the oil lamps. The saloon was buzzing—nervous laughter, clinking glasses, the piano player hitting keys a little too hard, stumbling through a tune someone barely remembered, and the smell of whiskey and leather tangled in the air.

No one stopped and stared like they used to when strangers walked in.

Cole walked in, calm as always, ordered a whiskey, and quietly took a seat. The whole room went still.

Deke Slater, Crowe's hotheaded lieutenant swaggered in. Deke was nursing a bruised jaw from Maggie's store, still burning with humiliation. He just couldn't resist the chance to pick a fight.

"Well, well. Look who thinks he's somebody. The tall stranger with more guts than sense."

He slammed his glass down and stood, hand hovering near his gun.

The room tensed. Every man knew it was about to turn bloody. The barkeep ducked behind the counter.

Cole just looked at Deke, steady, unflinching. "Don't do it, son. You draw iron in here, you won't be breathin 'long enough to regret it."

Deke sneered, his hand twitching. But before he could draw, Cole moved like lightning—back of his hand

65

cracking Deke across the jaw, spinning him into a table. Deke crashed down, dazed, his pistol skittering across the floor.

The saloon exploded with gasps. Cole didn't draw his gun. He just stood there, calm as ever. "Anybody else itchin 'to make Crowe's point for him?"

No one moved. The piano player started up again, nervously. The town had just seen something it hadn't in years: a man who didn't flinch when Crowe's name is spoken.

CHAPTER FIVE:
Crowe's Law

The ashes of Clancy's barn were barely cold when Crowe struck again. This time, he came bold as brass, riding straight into town with half a dozen men at his back. Their horses clattered hard on the boardwalk, iron shoes sparking as they pulled up in front of the sheriff's office.

Silas Boone stood in the doorway, hat in his hand, jaw tight. He knew what was coming.

Crowe swung down from the saddle, cigar glowing, eyes cold. "Sheriff," he drawled, loud enough for the whole street to hear, "looks like Copper Creek forgot who runs things. Time you reminded 'em."

Boone swallowed hard. "My job's keepin 'the peace."

Crowe stepped close, crowding him back into the doorway. "Then keep it. Enforce my peace." He shoved Boone hard, knocking him against the jamb. "Tell these people they pay my dues, they bow when I ride through, or they burn."

The sheriff shook his head. "I won't—"

The blow came fast, Crowe's fist snapping Boone's head sideways. Another followed, harder, splitting his lip. Boone staggered, clutching the doorframe, but Crowe grabbed his badge, tore it from his vest, and flung it into the dust.

"You ain't the law here, Boone," Crowe snarled, driving a boot into the man's gut and sending him sprawling. "I am."

Gasps rippled from the onlookers lining the street. Mothers clutched children, men looked away in shame. The sheriff — once their shield — lay bloodied in the dirt, coughing, while Crowe stood tall above him.

And if that weren't enough, Crowe's men turned down the street, finding their next mark. They dragged old Jonas Weaver, a small rancher, from his wagon, beating him bloody in front of his wife. One of the men slashed a knife across his harness, scattering his team and sending the wagon crashing into a trough.

The message was clear. Clancy first, the sheriff next, then anyone else.

Cole Hardin stood on the edge of the crowd, hands loose at his sides, eyes like coals. He didn't move, not yet — but everyone saw him there. And everyone knew Crowe's game.

This wasn't just about barns or cattle anymore. Crowe was daring the town to choose: keep bowing, or stand beside Hardin.

The street was still ringing with Crowe's voice when Cole Hardin moved forward. The crowd parted without a word, the sound of his boots on the boards sharp against the hush. He stopped between the fallen sheriff and the gang on horseback, broad-shouldered and steady as stone.

Crowe sat tall in the saddle, grinning down, cigar glowing like a coal. "Well now. The rooster struts."

Cole's gaze never wavered. "You've had your say, Crowe. Now you'll hear mine. This town don't belong to you. Not Clancy's herd, not Boone's badge, not Maggie's store, not a soul here."

A murmur rippled through the townsfolk — fear and hope twisted together.

Crowe leaned on his horn, laughing low. "Big talk for a man standin 'alone."

Cole's voice cut sharper. "Not alone. You beat down Boone, burned Clancy's barn, bloodied men who never raised a hand against you. That don't make you strong. That makes you a coward."

The word hung like a gun cocking.

Crowe's eyes hardened. His men shifted in their saddles, hands brushing holsters. "Careful, Hardin. Last man called me that's been pushin 'daisies ten years."

Cole took a slow step closer, his hand brushing the butt of his Colt. "Then you'll have company."

The street trembled on the edge of violence. Maggie Caldwell stood in her doorway, rifle in hand, Jesse beside her clutching his broom handle like a spear. Widow Hensley pressed her lips thin, eyes sharp. The blacksmith gripped his hammer.

Crowe saw it too — not just Cole, but the stirrings of a town long pressed under his thumb. He leaned back in the saddle, grin cold. "You think you've lit a fire, Hardin? All you've done is paint targets. Every soul in this town'll pay for your pride."

He jerked his reins, horse rearing. His men whooped and fired shots in the air before wheeling away in a storm of dust, leaving Boone in the dirt and the town buzzing with fear.

Cole bent, helping the sheriff to his feet. Boone's lip bled, eyes hollow, but when Cole pressed the tarnished badge back into his hand, the lawman's grip trembled.

"You still got a choice," Cole said quietly. "Fear, or fight."

The sheriff said nothing, but the weight of the badge burned in his palm.

The crowd whispered. Some glared at Cole, others nodded in approval. Either way, Copper Creek knew: the line had been drawn.

CHAPTER SIX:
A Stranger Becomes a Neighbor

The first week Cole Hardin stayed in Copper Creek, he didn't say much — didn't need to. He worked. He nodded. He minded his business. And folks noticed.

It started at the livery.

The morning was barely an hour old when Cole Hardin stepped through the open doors of the livery stable, hat tucked low, coat stiff from the road. Sunlight stretched thin across the dirt floor, catching dust motes that danced in the air like they didn't know there was a world outside.

Old Nate Curry was already up to his elbows in harness leather, muttering about cracked buckles and careless owners. His gray beard twitched when he glanced up and saw Cole.

"You're early," Nate said. "Or you're late, dependin 'what side of sleep you fell off."

Cole nodded. "Figured I'd see a man about work before the rest of the town woke."

"Town don't wake so quick anymore," Nate replied, going back to his stitching. "Crowe's had folks walkin ' quiet lately. Like they're afraid to make a noise someone else might notice."

Cole didn't answer right away. Instead, he tugged off his gloves, twitched a scrap of hay from his sleeve, and walked over to a brown-gold mare in the nearest stall. He held out a hand, palm open. The horse sniffed, snorted, and nudged his wrist in quiet greeting. With slow, practiced hands, he checked the hooves, then the flank.

"She's run hard," Cole said softly. "Left hock's stiff. Wants liniment and two days rest, unless you like lameness."

Nate stopped stitching, eyebrow raised. "You know your way around horses."

"Spent more time with them than with people."

Nate grunted, then finally set the bridle down. "That a fact. Well, most folks 'round here like a man who doesn't talk much." He paused, eyeing Cole a moment longer. "Name's Curry. You got one?"

"Hardin. Cole Hardin."

"You ridin 'on, Hardin? Or settlin'?"

Cole lifted his gaze to the farthest stall, where an empty saddle rested across a rack. His answer came quiet, but firm.

"Think I'm stayin'."

Nate nodded once. "What're you lookin 'for?"

"Work. Honest kind. Don't need much. Just a roof, a bed, and three meals when they come."

"That's all?" Nate snorted. "Men ask for less just before they ask for more."

"I don't ask twice."

The old man studied him for a long, slow beat, then jerked his chin toward a pitchfork in the corner. "You shovel those five stalls and feed the stock before noon, consider yourself hired. Two dollars a day. Don't mouth off at me and don't steal my tools. That's the job."

Cole nodded, rolled up his sleeves, and went to work.

As he started mucking the first stall, Nate watched him over the edge of his pipe. "Hardin?" he called.

Cole glanced over.

"You ain't askin 'questions about Crowe."

"Don't need to," Cole said. "I seen his kind."

Nate grunted. "Lot of folks 'round here did. That's why they duck their heads. Why they pay what he calls dues, just to keep cattle in the pasture."

Cole paused, leaning on the pitchfork. "Saw a woman yesterday give him coin she couldn't afford. Saw kids hush when they saw his riders. That ain't right."

"No," Nate said. "It ain't."

Cole went back to work. After a minute, Nate added, real low: "That's why I hope you really are stayin', Hardin."

Cole looked up, eyes hard and clear. "I'm stayin'," he said.

With that, he drove the fork down, turned the hay, and set the first change in motion in Copper Creek — quiet, steady, like it had always been waiting on him.

"You handle horses like a man who's been broke once or twice himself," Nate says.

"Difference is, I learned," Cole answers, cinching the strap.

Old Nate Curry wasn't one to talk unless a man deserved the air, but on the fifth morning of Cole mucking and mending before dawn, he finally grunted:"You show up before the sun again tomorrow and I'll start chargn ' rent for the air you're breathin'."

Cole paused, pitchfork in hand, and gave him the barest flicker of a smile. "Fair deal. Long as you don't charge extra for the dust."

Nate snorted, spit in the dirt, and walked away. But when coffee was poured an hour later, he slid a mug toward Cole without a word.

That was the start.

Two days later, Clara Penrose from the north pasture brought her cart into town, one wheel shaking so bad it looked ready to split.

"Just need to make it to the post office," she said, cheeks red.

Cole knelt beside the wheel, ran a palm along the shaken-spokes, and stood. "Ain't gonna make it ten feet."

Clara sighed. "Figures."

He didn't fuss. Didn't try to carry the burden for her either.

"Go get your mail," Cole said. "Wheel'll be fixed when you're done."

When she came back with two letters and a bundle of cloth, Cole was just tightening the last bolt. Clara blinked. "I didn't even hear you bring it in to mend."

Cole wiped his hands on his pants. "Didn't want to interrupt your errands."

She stared — and then smiled, small and stunned. "Thank you, Mr. Hardin," she said.

"Just Cole," he replied.

"Just Clara," she said — and rode off slower than she needed to, turning back once to look.

At Maggie Caldwell's general store, it was the broom that did it.

Jesse was sweeping the porch half-heartedly, dragging dust into a heap that the wind kept stealing back. Cole was leaning against the rail waiting for his coffee beans — and after watching Jesse fight the same leaf three times, Cole stepped forward, took the broom, and cleaned the porch in five effortless strokes.

Jesse stared. "How'd you do that?"

"Broom don't do the work," Cole said. "You do. And it goes where you tell it."

Jesse tried again. The broom listened better this time.

Maggie watched from just inside, arms folded, eyebrow raised. "You want a job?" she deadpanned.

Cole shook his head. "One's enough."

Maggie arched her brow. "And what's that job?"

"Livin'," he said. "Somethin 'I been tryin 'not to fail lately."

Something in that answer softened her, just for a second. She poured his coffee beans herself. And didn't charge him full weight.

By the week's end, folks didn't say "that stranger" anymore.

They said "Hardin."

Sometimes they said it with respect. Sometimes with curiosity. Sometimes with something like quiet hope tucked behind the words.

Cole didn't ask for that. But he didn't shrug it off either.

Because the truth was — he liked it here.

He liked the way Nate grumbled instead of thanked.

The way Clara smiled without meaning to.

The way Jesse listened like every word mattered.

The way Maggie stood like her store was a fort and she was the defender of all within it.

He didn't say it out loud — not even to himself.

But this town was starting to feel like a place worth standing for.

And that kind of feeling was dangerous for a man who'd made a habit of never staying put.

* * *

The dining room at Widow Hensley's boarding house smelled like roast chicken, fresh bread, and something faintly floral — maybe the soap she scrubbed the floor with every morning. The place was crowded tonight, every chair filled. The light came from three oil lamps and a pair of beeswax candles — soft and gold on the long table, making the dust in the air look like stars caught mid-fall.

Cole took the empty seat halfway down the right side, back to the wall out of habit.

The others were already talking. Laughter burst now and then — the kind that didn't quite shake off the week's tension, but came anyway, like flowers clawing through dry ground.

Widow Hensley herself set a plate in front of Cole — chicken, beans, and a generous scoop of potatoes. Her gray hair was braided tight behind her head; her sleeves were rolled past the elbows; her eyes, sharp as needles, didn't miss a thing.

"You want bread?" she asked.

"Yes, ma'am," Cole said.

She slid it over without ceremony. "You look like a man who's missed a few meals."

Cole nodded, picking up his fork. "Missed more than I should've."

"Well," the widow said, "you're not starving under my roof unless you mean to insult me."

That got a laugh from the table.

To Cole's left sat Ellen Briggs, the schoolteacher, petite and neat, with spectacles that seemed too large for her nose. Across from her was Harvey Jenkins, who ran the telegraph and had a fondness for boasting about how fast he could decode a wire.

And next to Harvey sat Mrs. Conklin, a heavyset woman who smelled of lavender and talked mostly of ailments — her own and others'. She leaned forward now, spoon poised over her gravy.

"You're a quiet one, Mr. Hardin," she said. "Been here a week and we've heard nary a word about where you're from."

Cole took a slow breath, chewed, and answered simply: "Wyoming. Near enough to the Snake."

"Oh my," Mrs. Conklin said. "That's wild country, isn't it? Indians and thieves?"

"Some," Cole replied. "Same as anywhere."

The schoolteacher leaned in, curious. "Did you grow up there? Do you have family still?"

Cole paused in the act of lifting his cup. Family. The word hit harder than he expected.

"No," he said. "Not anymore."

The table quieted a little. Widow Hensley glanced his way and nodded once — not with pity, but with understanding.

"So what brought you here?" Ellen Briggs asked. "Copper Creek isn't often anyone's destination unless they've got kin or business."

Cole hesitated. The room was warm, bright, full of voices and smells he'd grown unused to — places where people ate together instead of apart.

He set his fork down and answered honestly.

"Most places I go, I stay until I prove I shouldn't have," he said. "Figured I'd try the other way 'round this time."

That earned him a few stunned looks — and a small, knowing grin from Widow Hensley.

"Well," she said, ladling gravy onto her own plate, "stay as long as it takes to find out different, Mr. Hardin."

Jenkins leaned across, wiping at his mouth. "You planning to buy land? Start something? Or just keep working for Nate?"

Cole shrugged. "Don't know yet. I like horses, and quiet, and coffee strong enough to stand a spoon in. Copper Creek has at least two of those."

Mrs. Conklin chuckled. "Wait till you taste Ellen's coffee. It'll kill you faster than a gun if you aren't ready."

More laughter — this time a little easier.

Cole sat back, watching faces soften with shared food and easy teasing. He felt something hard in his chest shift — not gone, not healed — but loosened.

For the first time in a long while, he didn't feel like a man riding to his next goodbye.

He felt... almost still.

CHAPTER SEVEN:
Trouble in the Street

The table was being cleared and the last of the pie was gone when Cole excused himself. He stepped out onto the boarding house porch, the cool night air hitting him like a brace of riverwater. He'd forgotten how good stars looked when they weren't shoved aside by lanterns and trains and noise.

Widow Hensley's rocking chair creaked in the corner. The rest of the house settled into the soft night rhythm — floorboards, far-off cattle, a harmonica coming lazy from the saloon.

And then — that other sound.

Horse hooves. More than one. Coming slow. Too slow.

Cole turned his head, but didn't move otherwise. The men rode past the post office first, their shadows long and sharp across the moonlit dust. He counted three riders, maybe four — shapes too dark to make faces, but their posture said everything.

Not cowhands.
Not ranchfolk.
Men looking for something.

The lead rider pulled up in front of Maggie Caldwell's store. He tapped his horse's flank, looked around, and spat. Cole caught the glint of his belt buckle.

Big. Gaudy. Like everything about a man who wanted folks to *notice* him first and fear him second.

Cole stepped further into the shadows of the porch.

The men dismounted, weapons still sheathed but loose in the belts. They tried the store door. Locked. One of them thumped the window and grinned.

Cole listened.

"Looks shut up," one muttered.

"Doesn't matter," the bigger man replied. "Crowe said make sure *he* ain't here."

He.

Cole didn't blink.

They walked back to their horses. The man with the gaudy buckle swung into the saddle slow, scanning the buildings, street, and windows one by one.

His eyes passed over the boarding house porch.

Cole waited.

The rider smirked — cold as a shovel strike.

"Soon enough," he said, under his breath.

Then they rode off.

Their silhouettes shrank into the dark, and the night air returned to crickets and wind and the soft knock of Widow Hensley's screen door opening behind Cole.

"You seen something?" she asked, arms crossed.

"Figured you already heard," Cole replied, eyes still on the empty street.

"I heard," she said. "Question is — do you plan on doing something about it?"

Cole took a breath. "Depends what that something costs."

Widow Hensley gave a thin smile — sharp, but honest. "In this town," she said, "doing nothing costs more."

* * *

Morning hit Copper Creek soft as flour dust, carried on a breeze that smelled of oats and saddle leather. The town opened itself one latch at a time—storefronts creaking, stove pipes coughing, porch steps creaking under the weight of another day.

Cole was already awake.

He walked Maggie's way to return the empty coffee sack, nodding once to Eben at the smithy, twice to a ranch hand leading a mule, quiet enough to pass like a shadow.

Then the horses came.

Four of them, riding hard from the south road, bringing a storm of noise and dust behind them. Cole didn't move. Neither did the townsfolk who'd stepped out to sweep their porches or fetch water. They all knew those colors. That slanted posture in the saddle. That mirrored buckle glinting like a dare.

Crowe didn't seem to slow down until he was right in the middle of Main Street, reining in his horse with a jerk that sent gravel flying.

Two of his men flanked him. A third lingered at the edge, rifle slung low, watching windows.

Crowe chewed a toothpick instead of a cigar this time. He looked like a man who'd already eaten and was now deciding whether he wanted dessert.

"You good folks know why I'm here," he said, voice lazy, like it was all just neighborly business.

No one answered.

Crowe grinned — slow, sharp, ugly. "I thought I'd make something real clear." He leaned forward in the saddle. "You got a rat in your walls. Calls himself Cole Hardin."

A ripple went through the crowd. Very small. But it went.

"If he wasn't here, you wouldn't be sweatin 'bullets. " Crowe went on. "You wouldn't have watched a barn burn. Wouldn't have lost cattle. Wouldn't have needed to lock your doors at sundown."

A woman near the boarding house clutched her child tighter.

Crowe's eyes never stopped moving.

"You folks know me," he said. "I'm as reasonable as a man can be, long as his peace ain't messed with."

He shifted in the saddle, boot creaking, eyes gleaming.

"I only want Hardin. And if he's gone by sundown, everything goes back to the way it was."

Silence baked under the sun. A few people stared at dirt. A few looked at one another. A few looked at where they knew Cole was, even though no one was quite willing to name it.

Crowe watched their reactions like a man reading cards he already knew the ending to.

But Maggie Caldwell stepped forward. She folded her arms. Her jaw set."And what way was that, exactly?"

Crowe turned at the sound of her voice. "Lawful. Predictable. Quiet."

"You mean afraid," Maggie said, her voice cutting like a broom handle through glass. "You mean under your thumb. You mean your way."

A murmur followed her words — faint but real.

Crowe's smile didn't falter, but something behind it twitched.

"Y'know, Maggie. I admired your grit once." He leaned down. "But grit without sense just makes a grave deeper."

He looked around again — slow, savoring.

"Sundown," he said. "Hardin gone. And Copper Creek lives pleasant. Otherwise…" He didn't bother to finish the sentence. He didn't need to.

The message was nailed like a coffin lid.

The whole town watched as Crowe sat his horse in the middle of Main Street, throwing his threats like dice on a table everyone already knew was rigged.

"You got till sundown," he said, slow and satisfied. "Hardin goes… or this town remembers what it cost to forget who runs it."

His men smirked. Hands hovered over gun grips. A woman near the saloon door pulled her child behind her.

And then the front door of Maggie Caldwell's store swung open. Cole Hardin stepped into the street.

He didn't run. Didn't shout. Just walked — straight out where Crowe could see him, boots crunching gravel, dust lifting around his steps as if even the ground wasn't sure whether to hold him or let him go.

Crowe's grin stuttered. "Well," he said, leaning back in the saddle, "look what crawled out."

Cole stopped a few paces away — not close enough for a swing, but close enough that no one needed to raise their voice to hear the words that mattered.

"This town didn't ask for trouble," Cole said. His voice was calm, even — but every ounce of it carried. "They didn't ask for you. And they sure as hell didn't ask for me."

Crowe watched him, jaw working slow.

"But here we are," Cole continued. "And you can drag me or shoot me or hang me — but it won't stop what's already turning."

Crowe laughed — but it was thinner this time, the kind that starts with the throat and never reaches the eyes. "You callin 'yourself a martyr?" he said.

"No," Cole answered. "Just the start."

Crowe's face twitched — not at the words, but at the quiet behind them. The way the crowd had gone still.

People leaned out door frames. Hands paused mid-step. Widow Hensley stood stone still on her porch, one hand at her throat. Jesse hovered behind Maggie, eyes wide, breath tight.

Cole never moved his hands. Never touched his gun. Just looked Crowe in the eye like a man who'd already measured every cost.

"You want me gone?" Cole said. "You want peace, quiet, obedience? You'll have to bury me to get it."

Crowe gave a slow, soft clap — mock applause.

"That's what I figured," he drawled, voice turning cold. "One man thinks he's a spark, tries to light up the whole damn prairie."

He leaned forward in the saddle. "I'll put you down, Hardin."

"No," Cole said, stepping one pace closer, chin raised just enough to read as challenge. "You'll just prove I wasn't wrong about why you're afraid."

Silence snapped tight.
Crowe's men shifted.
Gunmetal gleamed.

And then — the preacher, Reverend Holt, stepped onto the church steps and said, "Enough."

Crowe didn't turn. "And who invited you, preacher?" he asked.

"The man you're threatening belongs to this town," Holt replied.

His voice had steel under it. "You want to drag someone out, you'll be dragging us all."

Crowe's smile slid off completely. "Then maybe I will."

He tugged the reins, eyes still locked on Cole. "Sundown," he said again. "You walk or they all fall."

He snapped the reins. His men wheeled their horses around. The hoofbeats trampled the morning quiet.

And Cole stood there until the dust settled.

Breathing. Watching. Deciding.

* * *

The low sun painted Copper Creek in fading gold by the time Cole finished stabling his horse that evening. The hitching post outside the livery was warm from the day's heat. Cole didn't notice much of anything anymore — just leaned against the rail, rolling the ache out of his shoulders and breathing the smell of sweat, hay, and old wood.

He didn't see Jesse until he'd already heard the footsteps.

"You ever think about teaching someone else how to ride like that?" Jesse asked, chin up, hands stuffed into his pockets like a boy trying to look older.

Cole didn't turn right away — just let a slow smile creep into his voice.

"You're askin 'if I teach?" he said.

"You're askin 'if I want to learn?" Jesse countered.

Cole pushed off the hitching post, met the boy's eyes. "Depends what you want to know."

Jesse hesitated. Then it came out all at once, like the dam had given way:

"Everything. Saddle work. How to mount without staggering. How to calm a horse when she's fightin 'the reins. How to keep your gun from catching on the strap. How you… how you just *look like you and the horse are the same thing.*"

Cole blinked once. Then reached for the nearest saddle.

"First rule," he said, flipping it onto the rail. "Horse don't trust the saddle until the man trusts the horse."

Jesse frowned, focused. "So what do you do?"

Cole showed him. Slow. Patient. Pressed a palm to the saddle horn, lifted slightly, then let it drop so the weight settled.

"A man who rushes this part winds up at the doctor, " Cole said. "Or worse."

He pulled the cinch strap free, held it out. "Here. You check the leather. Not your fingers. Let the weight do the talkin'."

Jesse took the strap and ran it through his hands the wrong way — too fast, too tight. Cole watched, then reached in and corrected the boy's grip. Not rough, but firm.

"Not like you're tryin 'to strangle it," Cole said. "Like you're lettin 'it breathe, see?"

Jesse nodded hard. Focused so tight he forgot to blink.

They worked like that for a while. Quietly. Like it was just a normal evening — like the town didn't fear every shadow. Like no one was waiting on someone else to make the first move.

But someone was watching.

From the porch of the general store, Maggie Caldwell leaned on the doorframe — arms folded, hair tied back, eyes unreadable.

She watched the way Cole stood — steady, patient — not barking, not bragging, just showing the work like it was worth knowing. She watched the way Jesse's face changed, like someone had finally taken him seriously.

She watched the way they fit together — not father and son, not teacher and student exactly, but something *that mattered* in a town that had gone numb.

And for the first time, Maggie didn't see Cole as a stranger. She saw him as a piece of something Copper Creek might need more than pride or prayers.

The shape of things was changing.

And somehow, without asking and without trying to lead, Cole Hardin was at the center of it.

* * *

Cole pushed through the batwing doors, tall and calm as ever. Conversation hushed as heads turned. He walked with that same measured stride, boots thudding softly against the worn boards, and stepped up to the bar.

"Coffee," he told the barkeep, his voice low.

Behind him, a chair scraped loud. Deke Slater rose, swaggering, a cruel grin tugging at his mouth. His hand hovered near his gunbelt as he called out, "Well, well. The big man himself. Thought you'd ride on out by now. Guess you ain't as smart as you look."

The saloon stilled. The piano player's hands froze above the keys.

Cole didn't turn right away. He lifted the coffee cup to his lips, took a slow sip, then set it down. Only then did he glance over his shoulder, his eyes like steel.

"I don't spook easy," Cole said evenly. "And I don't draw unless I have to. You aiming to make me prove it?"

93

Deke barked a laugh, but it was edged with nerves. "You think you're faster than me?"

He moved then—fast, hand flashing to his revolver. But Cole was already turning, already steady, his big hand resting easy on his gun though he hadn't cleared leather yet.

"Don't," Cole said, and there was something in that one word—quiet, certain—that froze the whole room.

Deke's fingers twitched on the grip. Sweat trickled down his temple. For a heartbeat, the saloon hung on a knife's edge.

Then Jed Crowe's voice cut through the tension like a whip. "Enough, Deke."

Crowe stood in the doorway, framed by the sunlight. He strolled in with that easy arrogance, every eye following him. "Not here. Not now. Man like Hardin deserves a proper finish, not some back-alley trick."

Deke scowled but eased his hand away from his pistol. He spat on the floor and muttered, "Next time, stranger."

Cole didn't move. He just turned back to the bar, lifted his coffee, and drank slow, as if nothing had happened.

But every man in that saloon knew—Copper Creek was heading straight for a showdown, and when it came, it wouldn't be Slater pulling the trigger first. It'd be Crowe.

And Cole Hardin would be waiting.

CHAPER EIGHT:
Town Hall

It was nearing midday when the storm of hoofbeats rolled into Copper Creek — not the forced, threatening walk from before, but a thunderous, deliberate entrance that sent chickens scattering and old men looking up from porches.

Crowe didn't come with three men this time.

He came with eight.

Guns low. Spurs biting dust. Eyes like stones.

He stopped in front of Maggie's store again, because that's where folks were used to talking, and talking was the farthest thing from his purpose now.

Maggie stepped out onto the porch with Jesse at her shoulder. Cole was nowhere in sight — though half the town figured he wasn't far.

Crowe didn't wait.

"You got one more chance," he called out, voice cutting across the street. "One more chance to make it right. I ain't asking where he's hiding. I ain't asking who's helping him. I'm telling you: hand him over or you start losing more than burnt barns."

He nodded once to his men.

One of them dismounted, pulled a length of rope from his saddlebag, and—without a word—began tying a knot. Loud. Slow. Meaning heavy enough to drag the whole street down with it.

Crowe kept going.

"You think a hero's worth the cost? I'll show you what a corpse is worth. Starting with the weak. The slow. The ones that don't shoot back."

Eben Talbot stepped forward then — arms like bridges of muscle and sweat. His voice was gravel.

"You lay a hand on anybody here, and you'll regret it."

Crowe smirked. "Good," he said. "A few regrets'll make what comes easier to swallow."

He pointed his finger — not at Eben — but at Clara Penrose, who stood stiff in the doorway of the telegraph office, hands clutching a ledger, eyes wide.

"Pretty thing like that gets snatched," Crowe said, voice cold and deliberate, "whole town will pay attention. Whole world might."

Maggie stepped down off the porch before she realized she was moving. Her jaw set. Her fingers curled into fists. "You're not touching her."

Crowe leaned low in the saddle.

"I won't need to," he said. "Not if you bring me the man who stirred this graveyard up in the first place."

Then — slowly, without breaking eye contact — he pulled his pistol and fired a shot into the sign above Maggie's porch. Splintered wood rained across the steps.

Jesse jumped.

Nobody screamed.

Crowe holstered the gun with a smirk. "That was just so you know the next bullet ain't goin 'into the roof."

He pulled on the reins, spurred the horse, and turned to go — but not before looking hard at the people watching from windows, doorways, and alleys.

"Sun goes down tomorrow," he said. "Cole Hardin rides out of Copper Creek alone… or I come back alone — and I bury what's left."

He rode off with the others, dust rising in a choking trail behind them.

And for the first time, Copper Creek wasn't silent because it was afraid.

It was silent because it was deciding.

* * *

Cole wasn't in town when Crowe made his move.

He was on the ridge just beyond the livery barn —

a low rise thick with brush and cut grass, a place he'd found by instinct the second day he arrived. A place where a man could look down over Copper Creek without being seen.

He stood there now, one hand resting on the saddle horn of his horse, the other clenched just tight enough to make his knuckles ache. From where he stood, the shapes in the street were small — but not small enough to miss the message.

He saw Maggie step down off her porch.
He saw Crowe blow the sign apart.
He saw Clara freeze in the telegraph doorway.
He saw Eben shift his weight, ready to throw down his life for something the whole town barely understood yet.

And he saw the rope.

The knot.

The man tying it.

Cole swallowed hard, jaw tightening. Not in fear. In the cold knowledge of what came next.

They're drawing battle lines, he thought.
And I'm the one they're being drawn around.

The sun was behind him, throwing his shadow long across the grass. A rider in stillness against a dying day. His rifle leaned in his saddle scabbard. His pistol hung at his side, grip worn to the shape of his hand.

He could have ridden down right then — cut through the scrub, broken into the street, stood in front of Crowe and dared him to finish it.

But he didn't.

Not because he was afraid to die.

Because dying now wouldn't save anyone.

Because if he came in guns blazing before the town was ready, the only thing left behind would be two bodies on the ground — and Crowe still in charge.

So Cole did the hardest thing he'd done since he rode into Copper Creek.

He watched.

He waited.

He made a choice with teeth in it.

"If I ride out now," he muttered, voice swallowed by the wind, "he wins. If I stay… maybe we all go instead."

A crow on the fence below let out a hard cry. A black shape against the coming night.

Cole turned and walked back toward his horse, boots cracking in the dirt.
One hand found the reins. One foot found the stirrup.

He mounted slow — not out of hesitation — but resolve.

If they decide I'm the cost, he thought, then I'll be the last thing he takes from them.

He turned his horse toward town — toward Maggie, Jesse, Holt, Widow Hensley, Clara, Eben, Nate — and the dozens of lives caught between one bad man's power and one good man's refusal to run.

* * *

The crowd didn't scatter far after Crowe rode out. They lingered, murmuring, their voices carrying sharp in the dry air. Mothers pulled children close, ranchers whispered in one another's ears, and before long, all eyes shifted toward Cole Hardin as he rode back into town.

It started with one voice — tight, angry.

"This is your fault, Hardin. You come ridin 'in, stir up Crowe's men, and now Clancy's barn is ash and Boone's beaten in the street!"

Others chimed in, voices rising like heat off the dirt.

"He'll burn us all out."

"He said as long as Hardin stays, none of us are safe."

"Best he ride on, and quick."

101

A knot of men pressed forward, not violent but insistent, pushing Cole toward the old meeting hall at the edge of Main. Jesse shoved at them, shouting for them to leave Cole be, until Maggie grabbed him by the arm and pulled him back. Her face was tight, unreadable.

Inside the hall, the air was heavy with dust and sweat. Half the town had crowded in, their fear louder than any gunshot.

An older rancher raised his voice. "Hardin, you're a marked man. Crowe won't stop till you're dead. And while you're here, he'll bleed the rest of us dry. If you've got any decency, you'll take your horse and leave."

A murmur of agreement rippled through the room.

Cole stood calmly in the center, hat in his hands, eyes sweeping the faces. He saw the fear, the anger, the desperation. But he also saw something else flickering at the edges.

Widow Hensley's voice cut sharp. "And what then? You think Crowe will stop if Hardin rides out? He'll just find another excuse. He'll take more until there's nothing left."

Tom Harper, the blacksmith, stepped forward, hammer still in his belt. "She's right. Hardin may be a stranger, but he's the first man in years who's stood eye to eye with Crowe and didn't blink. I'll stand with him."

The schoolteacher spoke up, timid but firm. "So will I."

Maggie's voice rang out, steady as iron. "You can blame Hardin all you want, but the truth is, Crowe owns this town because you've let him. Maybe it's time we stop lettin'."

The room split like dry timber. Shouts and arguments flew — some demanding Cole's departure, others rallying behind him. Sheriff Boone stood at the back, head bowed, saying nothing, the badge still heavy in his pocket.

Through it all, Cole never raised his voice. He waited until the room hushed enough to hear him.

"I didn't come here lookin 'for a fight," he said quietly. "But I won't run from one either. Crowe don't fear me — he fears what happens if you stop bowin 'your heads. You want me gone, I'll ride. But ask yourselves this: when I'm gone, who's next? Which one of you will Crowe break to remind the rest?"

Silence followed. Fear still hung heavy, but now it mingled with something sharper: shame, and the first sparks of defiance.

Cole set his hat back on his head. "I'll be at the Caldwell store if you want me. Decide for yourselves what kind of town you want Copper Creek to be."

He walked out into the sunlight, leaving the townsfolk to wrestle with their choice.

* * *

The fire at Clancy's ranch still smoldered when Crowe rode back to his camp in the hills. He sat his black stallion with a grin cut cruel across his face, his men trailing behind like jackals that had licked blood.

They gathered around the fire, dust and smoke rising as the horses stamped restlessly. Crowe dismounted slow, tossing his reins to Deke, the big brute whose nose still carried the crook of Hardin's fist from the store fight.

"Reckon you boys saw their faces," Crowe drawled, biting the end off a fresh cigar. "Clancy broken, the sheriff in the dirt, the whole town near beggin 'Hardin to ride on. Fear's a fire, and I just poured kerosene on it."

The men laughed, low and cruel, but Crowe's eyes gleamed darker. He leaned forward, smoke curling around his grin.

"Thing is," he said, "fear don't last if you let hope slip in. And Hardin's hope in boots. Tall, steady, never flinches. They're lookin 'at him like maybe he's the one to break me." His voice sharpened, flat and mean. "We can't have that."

One of the younger riders shifted uneasily. "He's just one man."

Crowe's head snapped toward him. "One man lit a fire in that town. One man made you three look like fools in Caldwell's store. One man got Boone to lift his eyes, if only for a second. You think I can let that stand?"

He flicked ash into the dirt, eyes glittering. "No. We'll cut Hardin down where everyone can see it. And we'll do it so they remember what happens when hope raises its head."

Deke grinned, showing broken teeth. "You want him dead quiet-like, or loud?"

Crowe's smile stretched slow. "Loud. Real loud. He's been sittin 'at that widow's boarding house, ain't he? Good. Tonight we take him when he steps out. Beat him, break him, drag him through the street if we have to. By dawn, they'll see him crawling, beggin', or bled out in the dirt."

The fire cracked, throwing sparks into the night. Crowe's men leaned closer, the promise of violence in their grins.

Crowe puffed his cigar, voice low, certain. "Copper Creek belongs to me. By the time we're through with Hardin, they won't just fear me again — they'll worship me."

CHAPTER NINE:
The Ambush

Copper Creek slept uneasy that night. The air was heavy, the streets too quiet, as if the whole town knew Crowe's men were planning payback.

The ambush came in the dark, as Widow Hensley's boarders slept. Cole had just stepped out to the pump, hat low, when the shadows moved. Six men closed around him, fast and hard. A boot heel scraped behind him — He staggered, spun, and swung. His fist crunched into a thug's jaw, dropping the man like a sack of meal. But two more lunged from the dark, clubs swinging.

Cole blocked one, but the second smashed across his ribs. He gasped, teeth gritted, and drove his elbow into a gut. The alley exploded into chaos — fists, boots, curses. Cole fought like a cornered wolf, landing heavy blows, sending one man sprawling into the mud. But numbers told the story.

A lariat dropped over his shoulders, yanked tight. He wrenched sideways, trying to break free, but another man smashed a pistol butt into his temple. Stars burst across his vision.

They drove him to his knees. One thug spat blood and snarled, "Crowe says hello, Hardin."

A club across the back of his skull, sent him sprawling into the dirt. Before he could rise, boots and fists rained down, each one driving him lower.

They tied his wrists cruelly behind his back, then looped the rope around his chest until it cut deep. Cole spat dirt and blood, eyes burning with fury.

They jerked the rope, dragging him down the alley like a prize steer. His boots scraped the ground, shoulders straining against the bonds. Each step hammered pain into his ribs, but he kept his head high, jaw tight.

In the hills near the edge of town, lanterns glowed. Crowe's campfire glowed like hellfire in the gulch. The camp waited, and with it, Crowe himself — a lean shadow seated on a crate, hat tipped low, cigar glowing red.

"Well, well," Crowe drawled as they dumped Cole in the dirt. "Look what we caught. Big, tall, proud Hardin. Not so steady with his face in the dirt, is he?You don't look half so mighty with your hands tied." He leaned forward, smoke curling from his grin. "We're gonna have ourselves a little talk, Mr. Hardin. And when I'm done, this town will know exactly who runs it."

Cole lifted his head, blood on his lip, eyes like steel. "You'll need more words."

Crowe chuckled, low and mean. "Don't you worry. I've got plenty."

The firelight threw Crowe's face into sharp planes, the cigar glow painting his grin devil-red. He leaned forward, elbows on his knees, every inch the cock of the roost.

"Hardin," he said slowly, savoring the name like a bad taste. "You walk into Copper Creek, stand tall in the street, and think that makes you king. You embarrassed my men. Worse, you did it in front of that shop woman and her brat. Now, folks are whispering. Whispering that Crowe ain't in charge no more. That burns me, Hardin. Burns deep."

Cole shifted against the ropes, blood drying at the corner of his mouth. "Maybe they're whispering 'cause they're sick of being scared."

Crowe's eyes narrowed. He plucked the cigar from his mouth, flicked ash close enough that Cole could smell it. "You think fear is weakness? Fear is control, Hardin. Fear keeps a town quiet, keeps men paying their dues and women lowering their eyes. It's the only law that matters. And I've been Copper Creek's law since before you even knew it was on a map."

Cole gave a dry laugh. "Funny kind of law. Sounds more like robbery."

The camp chuckled with Crowe — low, mean laughter, a pack of jackals. But Crowe didn't laugh long. He leaned closer, the brim of his hat shadowing his eyes.

They threw Cole against a post, rope looped tight around his chest and arms, pinning him upright. His breath came ragged, his ribs burning where boots had landed. Blood trickled into one eye.

Crowe rose from the crate slow, savoring the moment. He leaned on his saddle horn as if he were still mounted, eyes glinting. He backhanded Cole across the mouth. The men laughed.

"I'm gonna make you a lesson. Tomorrow, I'll have you strung up in front of Maggie Caldwell's store, rope tight around your neck. Folks'll see what happens when a man crosses me. They'll remember fear again."

Cole stared back, cold steel in his gaze. "Or they'll remember I stood up to you."

For the first time, Crowe's grin faltered. Just a flicker — but enough. He slammed his fist into Cole's jaw, snapping his head sideways.

"Careful, Hardin," Crowe hissed. "You're already a dead man. Don't make me bury you twice."

* * *

The knock came long after the lamps were out. Maggie Caldwell snatched her rifle from beside the counter, Jesse right behind her with a lantern. She cracked the door and found Tom Harper, the blacksmith, sweat dripping down his soot-streaked face.

"They got him, Maggie," Tom whispered, eyes darting over his shoulder. "Crowe's men. Dragged Hardin outta town not an hour past. Took him to the camp by the gulch."

Jesse's jaw dropped. "They caught *Cole*?" His voice cracked between shock and excitement. "We gotta do something!"

Maggie pulled him back by the collar. "Shut your mouth, boy. You want the whole street to hear?" She turned back to Tom, face hard as iron. "You sure?"

"Sure as sparks from my forge. They mean to string him up come morning."

Maggie slammed the door, heart pounding, rifle still in her hand. Jesse paced like a caged colt.

"We can't just sit here!" he burst out. "Cole stood up for us! He kept Crowe's men from roughing you up, from—"

Maggie cut him off sharp. "And if we ride out there with nothing but a broom handle and your smart mouth, Crowe'll hang us all side by side. You want that?"

Jesse's eyes glistened, fists balled. "I'm not afraid of him."

Maggie softened — just a fraction — then dropped the rifle on the counter with a heavy thud. "Afraid or not, boy, fear keeps you alive. But..." She looked toward the window, where Copper Creek lay quiet under the stars, its people cowed by Crowe's shadow. "...sometimes a body's gotta decide if livin 'scared is worth callin 'livin 'at all."

Jesse's head snapped up. "So we *are* going after him?"

Maggie pressed her lips into a tight line, then cracked a wry grin. "Looks like I'll need another broom."

* * *

Maggie Caldwell's voice carried sharp through the night air as she stood on the steps of her general store, Jesse at her side. A lantern swung above her, throwing long shadows across the dusty street.

"You've all been bowin 'your heads long enough!" she barked at the half-circle of townsfolk who had crept out of their homes. "Crowe's got Cole tied up by the gulch. At dawn, he means to hang him in front of us all — to show we're weak. You ready to watch another good man die while you hide in your houses?"

There was murmuring, shuffling boots. Tom Harper tightened his fists. His wife clutched her shawl. Jesse, standing straight as a fencepost, jabbed a finger at the crowd.

"He stood for us when Crowe's men came swaggerin 'in! You saw him. He didn't back down!"

And now he's payin 'for it! If we don't help him, then we deserve Crowe's chains!"

A silence fell — then a voice piped up from the crowd. "What can we do against guns, Maggie?"

She lifted her rifle high, firelight glinting on the barrel. "Plenty. Every hand here owns a tool that can swing or strike. Crowe ain't expectin 'the town to rise. He thinks we're all too scared." Her eyes swept them, fierce and unblinking. "I say we prove him wrong."

Slowly, one by one, the townsfolk nodded. The blacksmith raised his hammer. His wife pulled a pistol from her shawl. A stablehand lifted his pitchfork. Copper Creek, long cowed, was stirring awake.

Maggie's grin was sharp. "Then get yourselves ready. At dawn, Crowe's the one who'll be scared."

* * *

At the gulch, Cole Hardin stood roped to a post, bruised and bloodied. The fire crackled as Crowe's men circled like vultures.

One thug shoved a tin cup of water at him, only to yank it back and toss it in the dirt when Cole leaned for it. Laughter erupted.

Crowe himself leaned in from the shadows, cigar clenched in his teeth. "Still standin 'tall for a man who's about to swing, Hardin. You've got grit, I'll give you that. But grit don't win wars. Fear does."

He stood close enough that Cole could smell the tobacco and whiskey on his breath. "Come dawn, the

112

whole town'll see you hang. And when your boots stop kickin', Copper Creek will remember who owns it. Maggie Caldwell will remember. That boy of hers will remember. Every last one."

Cole spat blood in the dirt, lifting his head with a steady glare. "You're makin 'a mistake, Crowe. This town's done bendin 'the knee. And Maggie—" His lips curled in a half-smile, despite the rope cutting his wrists raw. "Maggie's got more fight in her than you'll ever stomach."

Crowe's face hardened. He drove his fist into Cole's stomach, doubling him over. "We'll see about that. At dawn, Hardin, you'll break — one way or another."

The men jeered. The fire popped. And above it all, Cole stood bound, battered, but still unbowed.

For hours, they worked him over.

Fists, boots, whips. They spit on him and hit him until his shirt was shredded and his body sagged against the ropes. Each time he started to slump, they hauled him upright and started again.

When the men tired, Crowe ordered him strung up — a rope over a tree branch, hoisting him so only his toes brushed dirt. His shoulders screamed, every muscle stretched past breaking.

"You see that, boys?" Crowe said, circling him like a preacher before a congregation. "This is what happens when you spit in my face. This is what Copper Creek'll see come dawn."

Cole rasped, voice raw, "You'll never own 'em all."

Crowe drove a fist into his gut, doubling him. "I own what they fear. And tonight, you're their fear."

They let him down only to start fresh. One man pressed a hot cigar to his arm, leaving a welt that blistered. Another doused him with whiskey — not to clean the wounds, but to burn. They shoved him into the dirt, stomped him down, then dragged him back to the post.

Crowe leaned close, whispering in his ear so only Cole heard. "You're not dyin 'tonight, Hardin. Not yet. You'll live till dawn, so I can hang you where Maggie Caldwell and her boy can watch. They'll see your legs kick, and the town'll bow again. You'll be the last hope they ever have — and I'll choke it dead in front of 'em."

Cole spat blood on his boots. "Takes more than you to break me."

The men roared, dragging him up again, but behind the cruelty, Crowe's eyes hardened. Cole was bleeding, battered, half-conscious — and still defiant. That defiance gnawed at him.

So Crowe shifted tactics. He stood in front of him, voice calm, cold. "You think you're savin 'that town? You're killing it. Every barn that burns, every rancher that bleeds — it's on you. And when they finally beg me to spare them, it'll be your name they curse."

Cole's head sagged, blood dripping into the dirt. But he forced his eyes open, met Crowe's stare, and rasped, "Then they'll curse me... for standing...."

Crowe's face twisted. He smashed his fist into Cole's jaw again, harder than before.

The night dragged on. Beating, hoisting, taunting. Each man took his turn until their fists were bruised. By the time the stars dimmed, Cole was barely upright, rope holding him more than his own strength.

As the first gray light of dawn crept over the gulch, Crowe lit another cigar, smoke curling like a serpent. He looked Cole up and down, his battered body trembling but still not broken.

"Enjoy the sunrise, Hardin," Crowe said softly. "It'll be your last."

CHAPTER TEN:
The Street War

The first rays of sunlight broke over the ridge line, washing Copper Creek in a pale, dusty gold. The street was already lined with townsfolk—silent, tight-jawed, waiting. They'd heard the word passed through the night like wildfire: Crowe was bringing Cole Hardin into town at dawn.

And there he was.

Cole stumbled beside Crowe's big black horse, his wrists tied to the saddle horn with rawhide, his shirt torn and dark with blood. Every step jarred his body, every tug of the horse threatened to drag him off his feet. But his back stayed straight. Even broken and bloodied, Cole Hardin refused to bow.

Crowe sat tall in the saddle, smug and smiling, as if he were parading a trophy. His men rode on either side, rifles slung loose, eyes hard. Behind them, the dust of the prairie still clung to their boots and coats, like smoke from some unholy fire.

The standoff held, taut as a drawn bow. Dust swirled in the rising sun, the rawhide pulling tight between Crowe's saddle and Cole's bound wrists.

A murmur ran through the crowd. Mothers pulled their children close. Old men muttered curses. A few of Crowe's hangers-on jeered, but even their voices cracked against the heavy quiet.

Cole's boots scraped over the packed earth. He lifted his chin, squinting against the sun. His eyes found Maggie in the crowd. She stood on the boardwalk in front of the general store, Jesse standing beside her. Her face was pale, lips pressed thin, but her eyes—her eyes burned steady, giving him strength he wasn't sure he still had.

"Morning, Copper Creek," Crowe called, tipping his hat, grin wide and cruel. "Thought you'd like to see what happens when a man gets it in his head to stand against me."

The sheriff stood there too, hat in his hands, sweat beading his forehead. Silas Boone looked smaller than ever, worn down by fear and compromise. But something flickered in him now as he watched Cole stumble—guilt, maybe, or shame.

The silence thickened. Crowe's men shifted in their saddles, smirking, waiting for their boss's next word. The town's tension was a living thing, crackling in the morning air, one heartbeat away from breaking.

Then, from somewhere in the crowd, a voice rang out—hoarse, angry:
"Why are you doing this?"

Crowe turned his head, smiling like a wolf. He leaned down on his saddle horn, eyes glinting. "Well, now. That's a good question." He let it hang there a beat, then raised his voice so all could hear. "Because as long as Cole Hardin stands up to me, none of you know where I'll strike next. I burned Clancy's barn to prove a point."

His grin widened. "And I reckon this here spectacle drives it home."

Cole swayed on his feet, his knees near buckling, but he forced out a few words, ragged and raw: "You'll pay… Crowe."

The outlaw only laughed. "Maybe. But first, you will.
"

The crowd swelled along Copper Creek's single dusty street—shopkeepers in aprons, ranch hands with weathered faces, women clutching children. All of them watching, waiting, their breaths shallow in the cool morning air. The only sound was the creak of Crowe's saddle leather and the scrape of Cole's boots as the outlaw's horse dragged him forward, step by punishing step.

Cole's head hung low for a moment, sweat dripping into the dust, but when he lifted it again, his eyes swept the townsfolk—measuring them, daring them. Some looked away. Some nodded almost imperceptibly, as if to whisper: *hold on*.

Crowe basked in the silence, smirking like a showman with a prize bull.
"Well, don't all thank me at once," he drawled. "I've gone and saved you fine folks from the trouble of deciding where you stand. This here's your example."

No one moved.

Maggie stood frozen on the boardwalk, Jesse at her side. The boy's fists were clenched, jaw tight, eyes darting between his ma and the beaten man stumbling in the dust. Maggie pressed her hand down on his shoulder, holding him back with all the force she had.

The sheriff, Silas Boone, hovered near the steps of the town hall. His hands twitched at his sides, his face pale. He wanted to speak, anyone could see it—but his voice stuck in his throat like a dry stone.

A farmer muttered, "We can't let this go on."

Another hissed back, "Quiet, you'll get us all killed."

The crowd rippled with that quiet argument, their courage rising and falling like waves against the shore.

Crowe's eyes glittered. He leaned forward in the saddle. "Which of you is man enough to try and stop me? Go on. Step forward. Let's see who's got the guts."

The silence deepened. You could hear the wind scudding dust along the street, the restless shift of horses, the faint rattle of a shutter on the saloon. Cole staggered but caught himself, standing as tall as his ruined body would allow.

"Don't reckon anyone's fool enough," Crowe said, savoring it.

Then it happened.

A single crack split the morning—a gunshot from somewhere in Crowe's line of men. Cole jerked forward,

119

his body arching as the bullet slammed into his back. He staggered, legs buckling, and hit the dirt with a grunt that silenced the street.

The shot hit like a hammer, driving him forward into the dirt. For a heartbeat he thought it was just another blow from Crowe's gang, until the fire bloomed in his back—hot, sharp, eating at his ribs. His breath caught, torn away, and the street spun sideways.

Dust filled his mouth. The ground was hard and cold against his cheek, but all he could feel was the throb spreading out from the wound, the sticky warmth soaking into his tattered shirt.

For a heartbeat Copper Creek froze. But the silence didn't hold. It shattered.

Maggie screamed.

That was all it took.

The town erupted.

Jesse charged first, pitchfork flashing as he rammed it into the flank of a thug's horse, sending the animal rearing. The rider toppled into the dust, where Tom Harper's hammer came down with a sickening crunch.

Gunfire exploded, muzzle flashes ripping the morning air. Bullets shattered the windows of the general store, glass raining down like ice. Maggie fired her rifle point-blank, dropping one of Crowe's men clean out of the saddle.

Cole, blood pooling in the dirt, rolled onto his side with a groan. His hands were still bound, but fury burned hotter than the pain. He kicked the legs out from under a thug who tried to finish him, dragging the man down into the dust.

Boots thundered around him. Screams and curses tangled with gunfire. He tried to lift his head but the world blurred, the figures moving like shadows in a storm.

Through it all, he caught snatches—Maggie's voice, sharp and raw, Jesse shouting his name, the sheriff bellowing though no one listened. He tried to push up on one arm but his body gave way, collapsing back into the dirt. *Not yet... not like this...*

His vision tunneled. Above him, the sky was pale and wide, a washed-out dawn already marred by smoke. The brawl rolled around him—Crowe's men trading bullets and fists with townsfolk who had finally snapped. He couldn't tell who was winning. Maybe no one was.

Dust boiled so thick it choked the morning light. Cole lay bleeding in the street, fighting to stay conscious as boots thundered past. The crack of rifles mixed with the scream of horses, the shouts of men locked in 99battle. The street was chaos — fists flying, townsfolk bellowing as years of fear turned into raw, righteous fury. Dust swirled in a cloud of grit and smoke. The thunder of fists and gunfire blended into one long roar.

Crowe himself bellowed above the storm, firing his pistol into the air. "Kill 'em all! Burn this town down!"

But his men faltered. For every shot they fired, a townsman swung back harder. A kitchen knife slashed across one thug's arm. Another was driven into the trough, half-drowned by two furious ranch hands.

And through it all, Maggie Caldwell stood tall, eyes blazing, rifle kicking against her shoulder. She planted herself over Cole's fallen body like a lioness, firing shot after shot, daring any man to come close.

Copper Creek had finally risen.

A shadow dropped to his side—Jesse, wide-eyed, clutching his sleeve. "Hold on, Cole! Don't you give up!" Maggie's hands yanked the boy back, but not before Cole caught the desperate plea in his voice. It sparked something—thin, but enough. He wasn't going to let Crowe win. Not here. Not with Jesse watching.

Gunfire cracked again, closer this time. Maggie cried out, dragging Jesse behind a wagon wheel. She fired again, dropping a man who'd gotten too close, then yanked Jesse down just as a bullet shattered the window above their heads. "Stay low, fool boy!" she barked.

"I ain't afraid!" Jesse shouted back, swinging his pitchfork at a rider's leg.

Someone cut the bindings from Cole's wrists and grabbed him under the arms, hauling him up, his body screaming with every jolt. He couldn't see who—it didn't matter.

The last thing he felt before darkness claimed him was rough hands lifting him, the world tilting, and the sound of Maggie's voice—steady now, commanding the townsfolk—"Get him out of here! To the doctor, quick!"

Then only the roar of his pulse and the black.

Crowe's laughter cut through the din, sharp and cold. He sat tall in the saddle, eyes blazing. "You think you can rise against me? This town belongs to me!"

* * *

The sun was sinking when Crowe's gang reached the ridge above their camp — riders slumped low in the saddle, dust clinging to sweat like shame. They dismounted slowly, trading grim looks, nobody speaking first. Behind them, Copper Creek sat quiet under the horizon, smoke from a few broken lamps or burning debris curling upward like ghosts.

Crowe swung down and handed off his reins. He didn't bother tying the horse. He walked straight into camp, every step sharp and certain. The others followed him, but not too close — some nursing bruises, others nursing their fear.

Calhoun limped toward the fire, using a split log as a crutch.

Flynn Mallory stood near the edge of the circle, shoulders knotted, heartbeat rattling hard against his ribs. He kept looking at the ground, at the others, at the saddlebag holding his rifle. Anywhere except at Crowe.

Crowe stopped in the center of camp and let the quiet settle, heavy and thick.

123

"You boys want to tell me," he said in a low voice, "why that town ain't ashes right now?"

A few shuffled feet. One man coughed. No one answered.

Crowe's eyes locked on Pike Granger, one of the older hands. "Say it," he ordered.

Pike swallowed. "We...uh...lost the crowd, boss. Folks fought back. Started throwin 'fists, stickin 'guns in our faces. Hardin got up and—"

Crowe turned. "Hardin got *up*?"

Pike nodded, cautious. "Didn't stay down like we figured."

Crowe's jaw flexed once. "And then?"

Pike hesitated, eyes flicking toward Flynn.

There was a pause. A long one.

Then Crowe's voice dropped, quiet as frost.

"Somebody shot without my say."

Flynn's chest tightened. The ground seemed to lean under him.

Calhoun flicked his eyes toward Flynn and mumbled, *"Told you he'd find out..."*

124

Crowe's head snapped toward him. "Calhoun."

Calhoun froze. "Sir?"

"You lookin 'at someone who knows somethin'?" Crowe asked.

Calhoun looked at Flynn for a half-second too long.

Then the dam broke.

"Saw Mallory shoot him, boss! Shot Hardin in the back without you sayin 'a damn word!"

Flynn snapped, "He was gettin 'up! I thought he had a gun—I panicked—"

Crowe didn't move. Didn't breathe. Just stared at Flynn, slow and still in a way that made the air feel sharp.

"You panicked."

Flynn nodded too fast. "Yes sir. I—I thought he was comin 'at you."

"So you shot him in the back."

"He—sir—he wasn't dead!"

Crowe closed the distance in two long steps. He didn't yell. He leaned in close, voice low and poisonous. "He wasn't down. He was standin' on his own two feet, tied to my horse You don't get to think when I'm standin '

125

in the street. You don't get to shoot till I say shoot. Because now? That town don't fear me." He jabbed a finger in Flynn's chest. "They're *angry.*"

Flynn swallowed hard. "Boss—I—I just—"

Crowe hit him so fast Calhoun didn't even gasp until Flynn was already on the ground.

Crowe dragged him up by the shirt and snarled inches from his face.

"You didn't kill Hardin. You didn't cripple him. You *woke him up.* And now every man, woman, and child in that town is thinkin 'about what it'd feel like to be him. Bleedin 'but alive."

He hauled Flynn forward and threw him face-first into the dirt. The others backed away.

"Dig," Crowe said.

Flynn lay there, breathing hard. "Wh-what?"

Crowe kicked a shovel toward him. Metal clanged.

"Dig your own hole," Crowe repeated, voice flat.

"You ain't gonna bury me—"

"I said *dig*, Mallory. You can stand or you can crawl, but you're startin 'a grave right now."

Flynn's hands shook. But he reached for the shovel.

Behind him, the others stood like gravestones — silent, pale, shaking.

And Crowe looked down at them with something close to satisfaction.

"This ain't about killin 'him," he said, voice loud enough for every man to hear. "It's about remindin 'every last one of you: I give the orders. I call the shots. I decide when a man lives or dies."

He turned back toward the west. Toward Copper Creek, now hidden by dusk. "That town thinks it saw the worst of me today," Crowe said quietly.

He smiled. "They ain't even seen the start."

CHAPTER ELEVEN:
Blood and Whiskey

They carried Cole into the back room of the boarding house where the doctor kept his practice — little more than a cot, a cabinet of bottles, and the smell of carbolic and whiskey. Maggie's face was pale but set, Jesse wide-eyed at her side.

"Lay him down," Dr. Hiram Keene barked, sleeves already rolled past his elbows. He was wiry, sharp-eyed, his hands steady. Cole grunted as they lowered him to the cot, the dark stain on his back spreading fast.

"Bullet's still in him," the doctor muttered, fishing forceps from a tin. "Maggie, boil water. Jesse — you hold that lamp steady or I'll box your ears."

The boy gulped but obeyed, hands trembling as he lifted the lantern. Maggie brought the kettle, steam rising as the doctor scrubbed his hands with harsh soap. He splashed whiskey over his fingers, then poured a long pull over the wound. Cole hissed through his teeth, his whole body bucking.

"Hold him," the doctor snapped.

Maggie pressed her palms against Cole's shoulders, firm and unyielding. "Stay still, Hardin."

Cole's breath came ragged, sweat shining on his face.

The doctor probed with the forceps, lantern light glinting on steel. The wound oozed dark, thick blood. Cole's fists clenched so tight his knuckles whitened. A groan tore from his throat when the metal scraped bone.

"Damn thing's lodged," Keene muttered. "Deep, too. Might kill him quicker to dig it out… but leave it, and he could die from lead poisoning."

"Then get it out," Cole ground out, jaw locked.

The doctor worked, sweat beading on his brow. Maggie kept her grip firm, whispering rough encouragement in Cole's ear. Jesse's face was pale, but his arm didn't waver with the lantern.

At last, with a sickening *clink*, the forceps dragged a blood-slick bullet free. Keene dropped it into a tin with a hollow ring.

Cole sagged, half-conscious, but alive.

"Not done," Keene said briskly. He poured more whiskey into the wound, ignoring Cole's ragged groan, then threaded a needle. Coarse stitches pulled flesh together, ugly but effective. When it was done, he packed the wound with clean cloth and bound it tight with strips of linen.

He wiped his hands on a rag, face grim. "He'll live — if fever don't take him. Keep the wound clean, change the bandage. If he burns up, pray."

Maggie squeezed Cole's hand once, hard. "He ain't burning. Not while I've got breath in me."

Cole's eyes flickered open, pain swimming there, but also the spark of stubborn fire. "Told you..." he whispered hoarsely. "...takes more than Crowe to put me down."

* * *

The doctor's footsteps faded down the hall, leaving Maggie, Jesse, and Cole alone in the lamplight. They had moved him to his room and laid him in his bed. Cole lay bound in bandages, his breathing shallow, skin damp with sweat. The whiskey and stitches had kept him alive, but the real fight had only begun.

By nightfall the fever set in. His skin burned under Maggie's palm, his sheets clinging to him with sweat. He tossed weakly, muttering words she couldn't catch.

The room was thick with heat, though the lamps had long since been doused. Maggie sat beside Cole's cot, wringing out a cloth and laying it across his burning forehead. His skin was slick with sweat, his breath shallow and uneven. The wound in his back was bound, but infection had its claws in him.

"Stay with me, Hardin," she whispered, dipping the cloth again. "Don't you dare let Crowe win by dyin'."

Cole muttered, his words broken and wandering. His head rolled against the pillow. "Dust... gun smoke...

130

can't... not again..." His fists clenched weakly, as if he were back in some battlefield only he could see.

Maggie pressed her palm to his shoulder, firm and steady. "It ain't gun smoke now, it's fever. You're here. With me."

From the corner, Jesse watched, eyes wide. He hadn't spoken for an hour, just sat with his knees hugged to his chest. Now he whispered, "Is he dyin', Ma?"

Maggie glanced at him, her face hard but her voice softer. "Not if I can help it." She held out the basin. "Bring me more cool water, and keep it comin'."

Jesse jumped to his feet, fetching the bucket from the well with a determination he hadn't shown before. His small frame staggered under the weight, but he grit his teeth and carried it in. Maggie gave him a quick nod before returning to Cole.

The night stretched on, broken only by Cole's fevered words. Sometimes he called out names Maggie didn't know. Sometimes he cursed Crowe's men in a whisper, teeth grinding against pain. Once, he said her name — not in delirium, but clear, desperate, like a drowning man reaching for shore.

Maggie's throat tightened, but she didn't falter. She kept bathing his brow, changing his bandages, forcing spoonfuls of water past his lips when he could swallow.

"Easy now," she murmured, wiping his brow with a rag dipped in cool water. "You hold steady, Hardin.

You've stared Crowe in the eye, you can damn well stare down a fever."

Cole thrashed, eyes half-lidded, and his voice broke ragged in the dark. "Don't… let him take… the boy—" His head jerked to the side, chest heaving.

Jesse swallowed hard. "He's talkin 'about me."

"Course he is," Maggie snapped, wringing out the rag. "Means he's still fighting in there. So keep that lamp steady and quit looking like a spooked colt."

For hours they worked — Maggie changing cloths, forcing sips of water past Cole's cracked lips, Jesse holding towels and fetching more cool water from the pump outside. Each time Cole slipped into silence, Jesse thought he'd stopped breathing, but Maggie's firm voice cut through.

"Not yet, Hardin. Don't you dare."

Near midnight, Cole lurched upright in a fever-dream, eyes wild. "Crowe! I'll kill—" He clawed at the air, nearly ripping his stitches. Maggie shoved him back down, straddling him to pin him.

"You'll kill yourself before you kill him, fool man," she hissed, holding him steady until the fever dragged him limp again.

Jesse stood frozen, lamp trembling in his hand. He'd never seen a man so broken down, yet still fighting with every breath. In that moment, something changed in the boy. Fear was still there, sure, but now it mixed with awe.

Jesse sat close now, lantern light dancing on his young, determined face. "I won't let him die, Ma. Not after what he did for us."

Maggie brushed damp hair from Cole's forehead, her jaw set. "Neither will I."

By dawn, Cole was still in the fever's grip. He lay still, pale and spent, but breathing deeper. Maggie slumped in a chair, exhausted, the rag still clenched in her hand. Jesse set the lamp down, eyes red but determined.

"He's gonna make it," the boy said softly. "He's too stubborn not to."

Maggie's eyes cracked open, voice hoarse but fierce. "That's the only thing saving us right now. His stubborn hide."

Cole stirred, lips dry, a ghost of a smile flickering. "Still here," he rasped.

Cole Hardin wasn't done yet.

* * *

The day wore long and heavy in Copper Creek. Maggie had sent Jesse down to the pump for water, a chore he'd taken on with quiet pride since Cole had been

133

laid up. The boy had grinned before leaving, tossing over his shoulder, "Back before you know it, Ma."

But the minutes stretched.

Cole, half-dozing in fever's shadow, stirred at Maggie's pacing. He lifted his head from the pillow, voice rough. "What's wrong?"

Maggie's eyes flicked to the clock on the wall, then to the empty window. She tried to sound steady. "He should've been back by now. Pump ain't but five minutes 'walk."

Cole's gut knotted. He shifted against the bed, pain burning sharp through his body, but he forced himself upright on one elbow. "How long?"

"Too long," Maggie whispered.

She was out the door a moment later, apron still on, running down the street. The pump stood quiet, the bucket tipped in the dirt, water long since dried to mud. Hoof prints scarred the ground beside it—fresh, deep, two horses, maybe three.

When she came back into the boarding house, her face was ashen. She carried the empty bucket like it weighed a hundred pounds. Cole knew the truth before she spoke a word.

"They took him," she said, the words flat, strangled, as though speaking them aloud made it real.

Cole pushed up further in bed, his body shaking with effort. "Crowe," he growled, jaw tight. The effort tore at his wound; he fell back with a gasp, sweat pouring down his face. He was too weak to ride, too weak even to stand—but the rage in him burned hotter than any fever.

Maggie set the bucket down hard, the wood cracking against the floorboards. Her hands trembled, but her eyes shone with fire. "He's just a boy, Cole. My boy."

Cole clenched his fists against the quilt, fury locked inside a body that wouldn't obey. "We'll get him back," he swore, his voice low, rasping, but full of steel. "Crowe doesn't know what he's started."

Maggie's chin lifted. "Then heal faster, Hardin. Because I can't fight this alone."

CHAPTER TWELVE:
Fever and Fear

Cole drifted in and out of blackness, fever dragging him like a river current. Sometimes he woke with the taste of dust still in his mouth, the echo of gunfire ringing in his ears. Other times he saw only shifting shadows on the walls, Maggie's voice cutting through the haze, sharp and steady.

"Drink this, Hardin. Come on, now."

She lifted his head, pressed a cup against his lips. The broth burned his tongue, but he swallowed because her eyes demanded it. Then he sagged back, sweat soaking the pillow, his body trembling under the quilt. The wound in his back throbbed like a branding iron.

When he came to again, the room was dimmer. Maggie stood at the window, hands clenched on the sill, staring out at the empty road. She hadn't said Jesse's name all day, and that told Cole plenty.

Silence hung heavy, broken only by Cole's labored breathing. He wanted to stand, to saddle a horse, to ride hell-for-leather after Crowe. But he couldn't even sit without falling sideways. The fever had him shackled worse than rope ever could.

"Maggie." His voice was low, steady despite the sickness dragging him down. "Listen to me. We'll get him back. But you can't go charging in alone."

She spun on him, fists clenched. "He's my boy! You think I can sit here and—" Her voice cracked, then steadied, hard as stone. "If you can't ride, I will. I'll storm that camp with my bare hands if I have to."

Cole managed the shadow of a smile, sweat dripping into the stubble on his face. "That's the grit I like in you. But wait. Give me time to heal. Crowe's expecting you to be rash. Don't hand him what he wants."

Maggie's breath hitched, but she forced herself back to the chair at his side. She wrung out the cloth and pressed it to his forehead, her hands trembling only slightly.

"You'd better heal fast, Hardin," she whispered. "Because Jesse's counting on us both."

Cole closed his eyes, slipping again toward the fever, but the last thought he clung to was Jesse's face. He would not leave that boy in Crowe's hands.

* * *

The house was too quiet. Outside, Copper Creek went about its business—wagons rattling over the ruts, dogs barking in the distance, the clang of a hammer from the blacksmith's shop. But inside, all Maggie could hear was the ragged pull of Cole's breath and the faint tick of the clock on the mantel.

He tossed beneath the quilt, skin burning hot one moment and clammy the next. Sweat darkened his shirt, plastering it to his back. When she bent close to wipe his brow, his lips moved, words catching in a hoarse whisper.

"Jesse... watch your back... Crowe's men..."

Maggie's chest tightened. She pressed the cloth firm against his forehead, willing him back to sense. "Hush now, Hardin. He's a tough boy. He'll hold on. You just worry about you."

But the lie tasted bitter. She hadn't slept since Jesse vanished. Every knock at the door made her heart leap, every hoofbeat down the street set her palms sweating. She'd scoured the edge of town herself that morning—pastures, pump, even the old mill—but there'd been no sign. Just those hoof prints in the dust, already blurred by the wind.

By afternoon, Cole tried to sit. He braced his hands on the bed, muscles trembling, teeth gritted against the stab in his back. Maggie caught him halfway up, cursing under her breath as she shoved him flat again.

"You trying to kill yourself?" she snapped.

His fever-bright eyes locked on hers. "He's got the boy, Maggie. Crowe's not gonna wait around. We don't have time."

"And what good are you like this?" she shot back, voice sharp as a whip. "You can't even walk across the floor, Hardin. You bleed out on me, then I'm burying you and still fetching my son alone. That's the truth."

Cole's jaw tightened, but he couldn't argue. He sagged back, chest heaving. Maggie stood over him, fists clenched, and for a moment the fight drained out of them both.

The rest of the day dragged. She boiled more water, changed his bandage, fed him sips of broth he hardly kept down. When the fever spiked again at dusk, she sat by the bed and held his hand, roughened from reins and rope.

"You've seen worse," she murmured, not sure if he could hear her. "So you hang on, Cole Hardin. Because Jesse needs you near as much as I do."

Cole drifted, caught between waking and dreaming. Faces swam in the haze—Jesse's, proud and scared all at once; Maggie's, lined with grit and fury; Crowe's, leering from the shadows. He tried to reach for his gun but his arm wouldn't lift. He heard horses thundering somewhere, a boy's cry, and then only Maggie's voice steady against the dark.

By morning, his fever had broken a little. The sunlight through the curtains seemed less cruel, and the cloth on his forehead cool instead of suffocating. But Jesse was still gone. That fact hung heavier than any fever, binding them both in silence as they faced another day of waiting.

* * *

Cole lay flat on his stomach, the smell of carbolic sharp in his nose and the slow ache of his wound pulsing with every heartbeat. Bandages tugged at his skin, stiff with dried blood, but the pain was dulled now, fading into something he could bear. The fever that had wrung him out in the first nights was breaking. He could think again, though the room tilted when he tried to sit up.

Maggie kept the curtains drawn against the worst of the midday sun. She moved quietly about the room, a basin of water on the nightstand, cloths folded neat as soldiers 'ranks.

"You're tougher than you look," Maggie said, wringing out a cloth. "I thought you'd be gone for sure when they carried you in."

Cole managed a thin smile. "Sorry to disappoint." His voice was low, raspy, but stronger than yesterday. "Crowe don't get the last word. Not while I've breath left in me."

Maggie's eyes narrowed, a flash of worry breaking through her tough mask. "That's the fever talking. Don't start planning revenge when you can't even sit a horse."

The words hung heavy in the room. Maggie pressed the cool cloth against Cole's forehead, her jaw set.

Cole stretched out across the narrow bed, back seared by a wound that burned whenever he moved wrong. He hated the helplessness. A man like him wasn't meant for lying idle while the world kept spinning outside.

Maggie refused to indulge him. She came and went like a storm—carrying trays of broth, swapping out bandages, scolding him for trying to roll onto his side.

"You keep twitchin 'like that, Hardin, and you'll tear those stitches wide open," she snapped one morning as she tugged the quilt straight.

Cole's lips tugged into a faint smile. "You'd make a fine nurse, Maggie."

"Don't flatter me. You're the worst patient I ever had, and I've birthed calves with more sense."

Her broom leaned against the wall by the door, always within reach. The sight of it made Cole's grin widen. "You planning to swat me back to health?"

"If that's what it takes." She folded her arms, leveling him with the same look she gave Crowe's men when they loitered near her store. "You think I've got time to pity you? You either fight to stand, or you lay there and rot. Choice is yours."

Cole's hand drifted toward his side, brushing the fresh bandage. He winced, then chuckled despite it. "You're a hard woman."

"Somebody's got to be," she shot back.

Their banter sparked like flint and steel. Maggie's toughness didn't grate on him—it anchored him. In her stubbornness, he saw his own reflection, the same grit that had carried him through years of hard trails. And slowly, with her goading, he forced himself upright, leaning heavy on the chair she shoved toward him.

"See? Not dead yet," she said, watching him sweat.

* * *

Jesse's absence was a wound of its own. Maggie tried not to let it show, but each time she looked out the window toward the hills, her jaw tightened. Crowe had him. That knowledge sat like a stone in her chest, though she kept her voice level.

CHAPTER THIRTEEN:
Jesse

The first thing Jesse noticed was the smell—smoke, whiskey, and horse sweat so thick it stung his nose. Crowe's camp wasn't much more than a circle of bedrolls and a dying fire tucked in a stand of cottonwoods, but to Jesse it felt like another world, a place where law and decency had been burned out of the ground.

They hadn't bothered tying him up, just dumped him off a saddle like a sack of grain. The fall knocked the wind out of him, but he scrambled up quick, fists clenched. One of Crowe's men laughed, cuffed him across the head, and shoved him down again.

"Look at him," the man jeered. "Little rooster thinks he's tough."

"Crowe'll like him mean," another replied, tossing a stick on the fire. "Might even keep the pup alive a spell."

Jesse bit his tongue. His head throbbed, but he forced himself not to cry, not to give them the satisfaction. He sat in the dirt, staring at the flames, listening as the outlaws passed around a bottle and argued over cards. Every so often, one of them would glance at him, grin, and spit in the dust at his feet.

By the time Crowe strode into camp, night had settled heavy. The outlaw dismounted easy, like a man stepping onto his own porch. His eyes landed on Jesse, sharp as a knife.

"Well, well," Crowe drawled, crouching so they were eye to eye. "Spittin 'image of your ma. Got her mouth too, I'll wager."

Jesse stared back, jaw tight. He wanted to spit in the man's face, but he held it down, knowing it would only earn him another blow.

Crowe chuckled low. "Don't look at me like that, pup. You'll learn. Everybody does." He patted Jesse's cheek, rough fingers lingering too long, then stood and turned to his men. "Keep him fed. Not too much. Boy's worth more with some fight in him."

The men laughed, but Jesse heard the edge in Crowe's tone. He wasn't a guest. He was bait.

Later, when the camp quieted, Jesse lay awake under the cold stars. His stomach growled from the crust of bread they'd tossed his way, his cheek still burned from that hand. He thought of Maggie's broom propped in the corner, of Cole laid up in bed swearing vengeance even with a bullet hole in his back.

He wasn't stupid. He knew his mother would tear the world apart to get him back. He knew Cole would come, weak or not. But he couldn't just sit here and wait to be rescued.

So Jesse watched. He noticed where the rifles leaned when the men slept too hard. He counted horses and who kept their reins loose. He listened to the rhythm of the watch—two men awake at a time, swapping near midnight. And he began to tuck little things away: a sharp stone hidden under his bedroll, a knot in the rope holding the water buckets, memorized paths out of the camp.

His heart pounded with fear, but underneath, something else stirred. A grit he didn't know he had.

Bide your time, he told himself. *When the chance comes, strike hard and run like hell.*

* * *

Out in Crowe's camp, Jesse played it quiet. He stacked firewood, fetched water, did what they barked at him to do—but all the while his eyes were sharp, measuring where the horses were tied, how the guards shifted, where the rifles leaned when the men grew drunk at night.

He thought of Cole, laid up in bed but alive. He thought of Maggie, who would never bend her knee to Crowe. And in his young chest, grit hardened into something more dangerous: patience.

Bide your time, he told himself. *When the chance comes, strike.*

* * *

The morning sun beat down on Jesse before he even stirred from the bedroll they'd thrown him on. A boot nudged his ribs hard.

"Up, pup," a gravelly voice growled. "Crowe don't feed layabouts."

Jesse blinked blearily, dust crusting his eyes, the taste of smoke in his throat. He wasn't at home. He wasn't at Maggie's table or helping Cole with the horses. He was in Crowe's camp, surrounded by men who stank of sweat and rotgut whiskey, their laughter sharp as broken glass.

One of them tossed a hunk of stale bread his way. Jesse caught it, scowling, but hunger gnawed too hard to resist. He tore at it with his teeth, chewing slow, glaring at the man who smirked back.

"That's it, pup. Eat up. We want you strong enough to squawk when Crowe drags you back into town." The outlaw spat into the dirt, then stomped off to fetch his horse.

Jesse's stomach turned—not from the bread, but from the truth in the man's words. He wasn't here for ransom. He was bait.

By midmorning, Crowe had him hauling water. The buckets nearly pulled his arms out of their sockets, the rope handles burning blisters into his palms. When he spilled a little, a man cuffed him hard across the ear. Jesse bit his tongue and kept walking. He would not give them the satisfaction of tears.

He noticed things instead.

- The camp wasn't guarded tight—just two men watching the edge at a time.

146

- The horses were hobbled, but not tethered close; a quick hand could free one.

- Rifles leaned against the cookfire log while the men argued over cards.

At noon, Crowe returned. He swung off his black stallion with the ease of a man who owned the world, and his men straightened, their jeers falling quiet. His eyes found Jesse immediately.

"Well now," Crowe said, stepping closer. He crouched down, his shadow long and sharp across Jesse's face. "Got your ma's stubborn look. I'll wager she's fit to tear her hair out by now. And that wounded cowboy she's coddling?" He chuckled darkly. "He won't last another week."

Jesse clenched his fists, nails digging into his palms. He wanted to tell Crowe that Cole Hardin was stronger than he knew, that his mother wasn't afraid of the devil himself. But the words jammed in his throat. He just glared.

Crowe grinned slow, straightening up. "That's it. Hold on to that fire. Makes it more fun when I snuff it out."

The men laughed as Crowe walked away. Jesse sat stiff, his ears ringing, his heart hammering like a wild colt's.

That night, when the camp finally settled, he lay awake staring at the stars. He thought of Maggie's voice, of Cole's strength. He wanted to believe they'd come for him. He did. But he also knew if the chance came, he'd have to fight his way out himself.

So he watched the guards change places. He listened to the rhythm of their boots on the dirt. He tucked a sharp stone under his blanket, hidden from sight.

Fear was still there, gnawing at him. But grit was growing too, steady and hard.

Crowe thinks I'm just bait, Jesse thought. *But I'll make him sorry he ever laid hands on me.*

* * *

The second evening, smoke from the campfire curled low under the trees, thick with grease and charred meat. Jesse sat on the edge of his bedroll, arms wrapped around his knees, trying not to breathe in the stink. His belly twisted with hunger, but he couldn't force another bite of the stringy rabbit they'd tossed at him.

Crowe strolled over slow, hands tucked easy behind his back. His men quieted as he came near, their laughter dying like snuffed candles. He crouched in front of Jesse, close enough that the boy could smell the whiskey on his breath.

"You've got your ma's eyes," Crowe said softly, almost kindly. "But you're gonna have to learn to see the world the way it really is."

Jesse glared at him, lips pressed tight.

Crowe smiled, sharp and lazy. "That cowboy you've been hangin 'around? Hardin? He's half dead.

Bullet tore him up bad. Fever's eatin 'him alive. He won't last the week."

Jesse's stomach dropped, but he forced his face to stay still.

"And your ma?" Crowe leaned closer, voice a low drawl meant for Jesse's ears alone. "She's too busy playin 'nurse to spare a thought for you. She's forgotten you, boy. Left you to me."

Jesse's throat tightened, his heart hammering. He wanted to shout, to call Crowe a liar, but his voice stuck fast. He thought of Cole's ragged breathing, Maggie pacing by the window. He knew they hadn't forgotten him—but the seed Crowe planted dug deep, twisting.

Crowe patted his shoulder, mock gentle. "Don't fight it, pup. Folks always choose themselves in the end. Best learn that lesson young."

He stood and walked back to the fire, leaving Jesse alone in the shadows. The men laughed again, passing the bottle, but the sound felt far away.

Jesse dug his nails into his palms until it hurt. *Don t listen. He 's wrong. They ain t forgotten me. Cole ain t dead. He can t be.*

But as the night dragged on, Crowe's words echoed louder than the crickets.

When the laughter at the fire rose again, Jesse turned his face away, into the dark. He dug his nails into his palms until half-moon cuts stung across his skin. But no matter how hard he tried, Crowe's words clung like burrs.

> Cole's half dead. Fever's eatin 'him alive.
> Your ma's forgotten you.

He bit down on his lip until he tasted blood. For a long while he held it back, chest heaving, eyes burning. But he was only twelve, and the weight was too much.

The first sob ripped free before he could stop it. Then another. Soon he had his face buried in his arms, shoulders shaking, hot tears soaking the dirt. He muffled it best he could, terrified one of Crowe's men would notice, but they were too busy with their bottle and cards.

Jesse cried for his ma, for Cole, for himself. For the empty chair by the kitchen table. For the buckets by the pump, tipped and forgotten. For the thought that maybe Crowe was right, that maybe he was alone.

But tears only went so far. After a while, he ran dry. His breathing slowed. His fists unclenched. He lifted his head and scrubbed his sleeve across his face, wiping away the salt and dust. The campfire had burned low, shadows deepening, Crowe's men stretched out in drunken heaps. The night felt still, waiting.

Jesse sniffed once, hard, and sat up. His chest still ached, but beneath it something else stirred — not fear, not despair, but a hot little ember that refused to die. He thought of Cole's voice, rough and steady even through fever. He thought of Maggie's iron jaw, the way she faced down Crowe with nothing but a broom.

No. They hadn't forgotten him. And he wouldn't forget himself.

He slid a hand under his bedroll and found the sharp stone he'd hidden. His thumb traced the edge until it nicked skin. Then, slowly, he leaned toward the water bucket rope. One careful scrape, then another. Fibers frayed soft under the stone's bite.

Not tonight. Not tomorrow maybe. But soon.

Jesse tucked the stone back and lay down again, his heartbeat calmer now, eyes burning but dry. Crowe thought he'd broken him. Let him think it. The real break was coming, and Jesse would be the one to deliver it.

CHAPTER FOURTEEN:
A Town Divided

The old clapboard church had never held so many folks at once. Every pew was packed, shoulders pressed tight, hats twisting nervously in calloused hands. Children clung to skirts, eyes wide at the sharp voices that ricocheted under the rafters. The faint smell of lamp oil and dust hung in the air, mingling with the heat of so many bodies.

It was near dusk, the last of the sun slanting red through the stained-glass cross above the door, when the meeting came to a head. Voices rose sharp, colliding under the rafters.

"We can't fight him," Jeb Colter barked, his voice carried across the pews "Crowe's got men, horses, guns. He's already got Jesse. Push him any harder, he'll slit the boy's throat just to prove a point."

A murmur of agreement rippled. Heads nodded. Some were too weary to argue. Fear sat heavy, heavier than the heat.

One man muttered, "Best to let it be. Crowe ain't never stopped till he's had his fill. If we bow our heads, maybe he'll leave the rest of us alone."

That struck a raw chord. Voices rose, overlapping, anger and fear colliding in the close space.

From the back, Maggie Caldwell's voice cut through, clear and hard. "That's what you've all been doin '—bowin 'your heads. And look where it's got you. Barns burned, pockets bled dry, the law in this town beat down like a dog. My son taken. "You think bowin 'your heads will save you? Crowe's been takin 'from this town piece by piece. You keep lettin 'him, and there won't be a Copper Creek left."

All eyes swung to her. She stood in the center aisle, her broom-hand hardened into a fist. Her face was pale, but her jaw was iron. "You think Crowe will stop if you give him ground? He'll take and take till there's nothin 'left. He's not leavin 'this town alone. You know it. So either you keep waitin 'on mercy that'll never come—or you stand."

The room crackled with murmurs, but many looked away from her fire.

A heavy silence followed, until a ranch hand named Saul Tucker stood from the middle pew. "She's right. Y'all saw Hardin stand in the street that day—shot to hell and still starin 'Crowe down. He ain't even from here, but he fought harder than most of us ever dared. What does that say about us?"

A few heads turned, shame flickering in tired eyes.

That was when Reverend Ezra Holt rose from the front pew. He was broad-shouldered, a man who'd swung an axe and run cattle before he'd ever opened a Bible. His hair was going gray, but his eyes burned sharp. He mounted the steps to the pulpit and faced the crowd, his voice steady as a hammer on an anvil.

"Maggie's right. And Saul's right," Holt said. "You all know it, even if fear's got your tongues waggin ' otherwise. Crowe's been runnin 'this town like it's his own spread. But Copper Creek belongs to God Almighty and to those willing to defend it."

The room hushed. Holt leaned both hands on the pulpit, shoulders taut.

"I'm no young man," he went on, "but I can still hold a rifle straight. I've buried friends, and I'll be damned before I bury this town because we were too scared to lift our heads."

His words cracked something in the silence. Old farmer Eben Tate stood, holding a battered shotgun across his chest. "Reverend's right. I'll fight. Better to die standin 'than livin 'on my knees."

Mary Lou, the seamstress, rose next, her lantern pole clutched tight. "Crowe's already taken Jesse. But he's taken from every one of us. I won't sit by no longer."

The blacksmith raised his hammer. A schoolteacher lifted a kitchen knife.

Still, fear clung. Jeb Colter pointed a shaking finger. "You'll all be corpses. Crowe'll cut you down like wheat. And when he does, don't you look to me."

"Better cut down standin 'than crawlin'," Maggie shot back, her voice like a whip.

Reverend Holt stepped down from the pulpit, standing shoulder to shoulder with her. "Jeb, you can go home and wait for Crowe to come to your door. The rest of us—we're done waiting."

And then it spread. One by one, townsfolk stood. Not all. Not even half. But enough. A handful gathered at the front—men and women with shotguns, rifles, hammers, knives, and grit. Reverend Holt laid a hand on each shoulder as if blessing them.

"We ain't soldiers," he said, his voice carrying to the rafters. "But we are Copper Creek. Tonight, we stop bein 'Crowe's victims. Tonight, we stand as a militia."

The word hung in the air, raw but alive.

As the lamps guttered and folk filed into the night, those who pledged stayed close, their faces set. Maggie stood among them, her eyes fierce, her shoulders squared, but her presence alone was steel.

For the first time in too long, Copper Creek had chosen defiance. Crowe had Jesse, but the town had found its backbone.

* * *

Cole stirred at the scrape of boots on the floorboards. His fever had broken enough that he knew night from day again, though pain still burned hot in his back. He turned his head on the pillow, blinking through the dim lamplight as Maggie slipped into the room.

Her hair was damp with sweat, her face pale but lit with something fierce. She carried no broom tonight—just that fire in her eyes.

"You've been out again," Cole rasped, his voice low and hoarse.

Maggie dropped into the chair by the bed. For a long moment, she just stared at him, chest rising and falling like she'd come from a fight. Then she leaned forward, her voice clipped, urgent. "We met in the church. The town. Most came. Half of 'em still want to bow, half of 'em too scared to move—but some stood. Enough to matter."

Cole pushed against the mattress, fighting to sit. His muscles quivered with effort, sweat beading on his brow. "Enough... for what?"

"For a militia," Maggie said. Her hands clenched on her knees. "Reverend Holt led it. Called us Copper Creek's militia right there at the pulpit. Eben Tate, Mary Lou, the blacksmith, a few others. We're ragged, but we're standin'."

Cole let the words sink in. His throat worked, but no sound came at first. He looked at her, at the defiance etched in every line of her face, and felt a sting of shame burn hotter than his wound.

"You don't need me," he muttered finally.

Maggie's eyes narrowed. "Don't be a damn fool."

"I can't even stand," Cole growled. He gestured weakly at his bandaged back. "What good's a man in bed when there's fight brewin 'in the street?"

"You're the good you showed 'em already." Her voice cut like steel. "You think they rose up on their own? They saw you face Crowe when nobody else would. You lit the fire, Hardin. You don't get to crawl back under the ashes now."

He stared at her, chest heaving. Shame warred with stubborn pride. Fever still blurred the edges of the room, but her words cut through clean.

"I should be out there," he said, softer now.

"And you will be," Maggie shot back. "But you'll do it on your feet, not carried in a box. Until then, you heal. That's your part in this fight tonight."

Cole closed his eyes, his jaw tight. He hated the truth in her words, hated his own weakness. But beneath the hate, something else stirred—a slow, stubborn resolve.

When he opened his eyes again, he found Maggie watching him, her hand resting light on the bed frame. For the first time since the bullet dropped him, he felt more than pain. He felt the weight of what was coming.

"I'll heal," he swore, voice ragged but steady. "And when I do, Crowe's gonna pay."

Maggie leaned back, her shoulders easing just a hair. "That's more like it."

The lamp flickered low, making shadows across the walls, and in the stillness between them, Copper Creek's fight began to feel real.

* * *

The days bled together in heat and pain. Cole drifted in and out, fever breaking at last but leaving him hollowed, weak as a colt on its first legs. The bullet wound burned with every breath, and the ache in his ribs spread through his whole body like fire under his skin.

Maggie never let him wallow.

Morning found her at his side with broth, her expression carved from stone. "Sit up," she ordered, tugging the pillows into place behind him.

Cole grimaced, trying to brace himself with one arm. The muscles in his back spasmed and he collapsed with a sharp hiss.

"Try again," Maggie said flatly.

He shot her a glare, but her eyes didn't waver. Gritting his teeth, he pressed harder, sweat breaking on his brow. Inch by inch, he rose until he was half upright, trembling all over.

Maggie slid the cup into his hands. "There. You're not as helpless as you pretend."

The broth scalded his tongue, thin but rich enough to give him strength. He drained it slow, his jaw tight against the tremor in his arms. When he lowered the cup, Maggie took it without a word, refilled it, and set it back in his hands.

"You treat me like a calf that needs breaking," Cole muttered.

Maggie's mouth twitched, but her eyes stayed sharp. "I treat you like a man too damn stubborn to know he ain't dead yet."

By evening, she had him on his feet, one arm slung across her shoulders. His legs shook, knees buckling as she dragged him toward the window. The light slanted gold across the street, where children played in the dust, their laughter brittle under the shadow of Crowe's name.

Cole gritted his teeth, straightening his spine. His body screamed, but he forced himself to stand tall, if only for a heartbeat. Maggie steadied him, her breath hard in her chest.

"That's it," she said, softer now. "One step at a time."

He sagged back onto the bed, drenched in sweat, but a flicker of pride cut through the pain.

Later that night, the fever dreams came again— dusty streets, Crowe's laughter, Jesse's face vanishing into smoke. He woke thrashing, gasping for breath. Maggie pinned him with both hands, forcing him back down.

"Easy, Hardin. Easy," she murmured, voice steady even as her eyes glistened. "It's just the fever. You're here. You're alive."

Cole caught her wrist, his grip weak but desperate. "Jesse…"

Her jaw tightened, and she pressed her free hand against his chest. "We'll get him back. You just keep breathing till you can hold a gun again."

Cole let go, sinking back into the mattress. His body ached, but his resolve burned sharper. He would not die in this bed. Not while Jesse was out there, not while Crowe strutted through Copper Creek like a king.

And Maggie—tough, relentless Maggie—wouldn't let him.

CHAPTER FIFTEEN:
Crowe's Fury

The campfire snapped and popped, sparks leaping into the night. Jesse sat close enough to feel the heat but not enough to be warmed. One of Crowe's men had shoved a tin plate of beans into his hands, but most had gone cold while he stared at the fire, lost in thought.

The men were in high spirits, passing a bottle back and forth, trading filthy jokes. Jesse kept his head down, trying to disappear into the shadows. But his ears were sharp.

"Copper Creek's riled up," one outlaw muttered, tugging at the cards in his hand.

Another snorted. "A handful of farmers with squirrel guns? Let 'em come. Crowe'll cut 'em to ribbons."

Jesse's stomach turned, but he kept still.

Then Crowe himself strode into the circle, black hat pulled low, the fire catching the edge of his grin. He didn't sit. He just stood there, looming, his presence enough to quiet the camp.

"They think they've found a backbone," Crowe said. His voice was soft, but it carried. "Met in the church, called themselves a militia." He laughed, slow and cruel. "They forget I've already got the only leverage I need."

His eyes slid toward Jesse. The men chuckled.

Crowe went on, pacing now, boots grinding into the dirt. "We'll let 'em build their courage. Let 'em polish their rifles, pray their little prayers. And when they're good and ready, we'll ride in and smash the lot. Burn the store, hang their preacher, and drag Hardin out of his sickbed to finish what I started."

Jesse froze. His heart pounded so hard he thought they'd hear it.

Crowe's eyes cut back to him, sharp as a knife. "Boy, you'll be right there in the street when it happens. Watchin 'your ma beg. Watchin 'Hardin bleed again. And you'll learn what happens to fools who think they can fight me."

The men howled with laughter. Crowe tipped his hat low, the firelight glinting off his teeth, then stalked back into the dark.

Jesse's hands shook, the tin plate rattling in his lap. He shoved it aside, curling his fists tight to stop the trembling. Tears threatened, but he swallowed them down.

They're gonna burn Copper Creek.

His mind raced. He couldn't sit and wait to be used as bait. He had to warn them. He had to find a way out.

As the camp settled into drunken snores, Jesse slid his hand under his bedroll and found the stone again. His thumb pressed hard against the edge, skin breaking, blood slicking his palm. It steadied him.

I'll get free. I'll get back. They'll know what's coming.

For the first time, his fear gave way to something fiercer. A spark that felt bigger than himself.

* * *

The camp lay quiet, only the hiss of the fire and the low groans of drunk men turning in their sleep. The horses stamped in the shadows, tails flicking at gnats, the leather of their tack creaking as they shifted.

Jesse lay stiff on his bedroll, every muscle tight, heart hammering so loud he thought it might wake them. He stared up at the stars through the trees, replaying Crowe's words in his head. *Burn the store. Hang the preacher. Drag Hardin out to die.*

He couldn't let that happen. He had to get free.

His fingers crept under the blanket and found the sharp stone. He curled it in his palm, the edge digging into his skin until he drew courage from the sting. He glanced at the nearest outlaw—slumped over, snoring, hat tilted low. The rifle that had been in his hands earlier leaned careless against a stump.

This was it.

Jesse's breath came shallow as he slid out from under the blanket, moving inch by inch across the dirt. His knees sank into the dust, his hands shaking so badly the stone nearly slipped. He reached the rope that tied the water buckets, frayed already from his secret scraping. He sawed at it now, desperate, fast but trying to stay quiet. Fibers snapped one by one.

The rope gave with a faint pop. One bucket toppled, clanging against a rock.

Jesse froze, blood roaring in his ears. One of the men stirred, muttered, and rolled over. The campfire crackled, covering the sound. Jesse held his breath until his chest ached, then moved again, crawling toward the horses.

The animals shifted nervously as he neared. He reached out, fingers fumbling at a hobble knot. It was stiff, caked with dust and sweat. He worked at it with the stone, sawing, his breath ragged. The leather gave an inch, then two.

A horse snorted and jerked its head, ears flicking. Jesse's stomach dropped. He froze again, praying.

Then a hand clamped his shoulder. "Where d'you think you're goin', pup?"

Rough fingers yanked him upright. Jesse's cry tore through the camp, snapping the men awake. Boots thudded, curses filled the night, and in an instant, Jesse was ringed in torchlight and grinning faces.

The outlaw who caught him shoved him forward into the dirt. "Told you he'd try somethin'. Little rooster's got claws."

Crowe appeared from the shadows, black hat low, smile cold. He crouched beside Jesse, lifting his chin with one finger.

"Thought you'd play hero, did you? Thought you'd run squealin 'back to mama?" His voice was soft, cruel. "I admire the spirit. But spirit needs breakin'."

He nodded once, and two men hauled Jesse up, pinning his arms as he kicked and thrashed. The firelight glinted off Crowe's teeth as he leaned close.

"Next time you think of runnin', boy, remember this night."

The men dragged Jesse back to his bedroll, tied his wrists tight with rawhide, and left him under watch. His arms ached, his cheeks burned with dirt and tears.

But as he lay there staring at the fire, chest heaving, Jesse swallowed hard and clenched his jaw. They'd caught him this time. They'd punish him. But they hadn't broken him.

And next time—he swore—he wouldn't fail.

* * *

Morning broke gray, a weak light bleeding through the cottonwoods. Jesse's wrists ached from the rawhide thongs that bound him, his shoulders stiff, his mouth dry as dust. He'd barely slept. Every time he drifted, Crowe's smile rose out of the dark like a brand.

The camp stirred with curses and the scrape of boots. Horses stamped, the smell of frying bacon drifted over the fire. Then a stir went through the men— someone was being dragged in.

Jesse craned his neck, heart pounding. Two outlaws hauled a farmer into the circle, his clothes torn, his lip split. Jesse recognized him—Zeke Avery, a quiet man from a spread outside town. He'd seen him in Maggie's store more than once.

Crowe appeared from his tent, hat low, coat flaring behind him. His eyes swept the camp, then fixed on Jesse. A slow grin spread across his face.

"Seems we caught us a rat," he drawled, jerking his chin toward Avery. "This one was sniffin 'around the edge of camp. Tryin 'to bring word back to Maggie Callahan and her preacher."

The farmer shook his head, blood on his teeth. "I just came for my son's mare. She strayed—"

Crowe silenced him with a backhand that sent him sprawling. He drew his Colt and thumbed the hammer back with a click that froze the whole camp.

"You think I'll let anyone play spy? You think you can run to that church and whisper in their ears?" Crowe's voice was soft but carried, every word meant for Jesse. "This is what happens to folks who cross me."

He leveled the gun at Avery's chest.

"Wait—" Jesse heard himself shout, his voice cracking. But it was too late.

The pistol roared. Avery jerked once, then crumpled in the dust, smoke rising from the wound. The smell of blood and gunpowder hung heavy, sharper than the bacon, thicker than the morning air.

The camp went still. Some of the men cheered low, savage grins splitting their faces. But Jesse saw others glance away, their jaws tight, eyes shadowed.

One of the younger riders spat into the dirt and muttered, "Weren't no spy."
Another hissed at him to shut up.

Crowe holstered his gun, calm as if he'd swatted a fly. He turned, his gaze pinning Jesse like a nail. "Remember this, pup. This is the cost of resistance. Next time your ma or that preacher get ideas, picture this man rottin 'in the dirt. That's what defiance buys."

The outlaws dragged Avery's body toward the trees. The camp slowly returned to its rhythm, though the laughter was forced, brittle.

Jesse's throat burned, his stomach twisted. He'd seen death before, but never like this—cold, deliberate, staged like a sermon. He wanted to curl into himself, to shut it out. But instead he forced his eyes open, watching everything.

And he saw it.

The way some of Crowe's men shifted uneasily. The way one grumbled under his breath, silenced by a sharper glare. The cracks.

Crowe ruled with fear, but fear didn't bind as tight as loyalty. Jesse tucked that knowledge away, the stone of his resolve grinding sharper.

They could kill a farmer. They could beat him bloody. But he would not give Crowe the satisfaction of breaking.

* * *

Jesse couldn't get the sound of the gunshot out of his ears. It rang in him all morning, a sharp crack that seemed to split the world in two. The farmer's body had been dragged into the brush, but the image of him falling — his eyes wide, his chest blooming red — stayed burned in Jesse's mind.

The men tried to act like nothing had happened. They ate, they joked, they spat into the dirt. But Jesse saw it now — the cracks Crowe hadn't meant to show him.

At breakfast, two of the gang argued low over who was supposed to watch the camp.

"You saw him sneakin'," one muttered.

"I saw a man lookin 'for a horse," the other snapped back. "That ain't the same as spyin'."

A third man cut in with a sneer. "Crowe says it's betrayal, it's betrayal. Don't matter what you saw."

The first man fell silent, but his jaw worked, tight as a vise.

Later, Jesse fetched water with his wrists unbound — under watch, but not tied. He staggered under the weight of the buckets, but his ears were sharp.

Behind him, two men squatted near the fire, cleaning their pistols.

"Crowe's gone too far," one grumbled. "Shootin 'a man in cold blood? That'll stir the town worse, not scare 'em quiet."

"You keep your damn mouth shut," the other hissed, though his hands shook as he reassembled the cylinder.

Jesse pretended not to hear, but inside, something flickered. Crowe's cruelty worked like a whip, but not everyone wanted to be lashed forever. Fear had them by the throat, but fear could break.

That night, Jesse tested the edges of his bonds when they tied him again. He'd hidden a sliver of sharp stone in his boot — risked everything to slip it there while the men laughed over cards. As the fire burned low and snores rose around him, he sawed carefully at the rawhide. It held, but the fibers frayed a little under his work.

He froze when a guard shifted, muttering in his sleep. Jesse held his breath until the man settled, then worked another moment, heart thundering. Not tonight. But maybe soon.

Lying back, he stared at the stars through the trees. He thought of Cole, fevered but unbroken. He thought of Maggie, standing in the church with fire in her voice. Crowe wanted him scared and hopeless. But Jesse was learning.

169

He was learning who flinched at Crowe's orders. Who grumbled after the farmer fell. Who drank too much at night and left rifles leaning easy against stumps.

The cracks were there. He just had to be smart enough, and patient enough, to wedge them open.

CHAPTER SIXTEEN:
Hardin Rises Again

The sun was dropping low, painting Copper Creek in shades of gold and dust. Behind the clapboard church, the townsfolk who had stood in defiance gathered in a nervous knot. Men clutched old rifles that hadn't fired in years, women carried lantern poles and axes. Some had pistols tucked in belts that looked too loose for the weight.

Reverend Holt stood tall at the front, sleeves rolled past his elbows, the lines in his face deep but not defeated. He looked less preacher than ranch hand tonight, a shotgun cradled easy in his arms.

"All right," he said, his voice carrying over the murmurs. "You're a militia now. That means you learn to act like one. First lesson—discipline. You move when I tell you, not when your nerves say run."

The blacksmith gave a grunt, trying to square his shoulders like a soldier. Mary Lou gripped her lantern pole so tight her knuckles went white. Eben Tate fiddled with the trigger of his battered shotgun until Holt barked at him to keep it steady.

They tried to march in a line, boots scuffing, faces red. They fired a few rounds into a stump, the shots ragged, echoing off the hills. Every missed mark and crooked stance showed just how unready they were. Yet when Holt barked praise, pride flickered in their eyes.

Maggie walked the line like a sergeant, sharp-tongued, broom in hand as if daring anyone to laugh at her weapon. "Stand tall, you lot," she snapped at one rancher who hunched low. "Crowe's men'll smell fear before they see your face. You want to look beat, you might as well dig your own grave."

They straightened under her gaze. She was no soldier, but her fire carried more weight than any drill command.

Cole heard the faint crack of rifles in the distance. He lay on his stomach, the bandages on his back freshly changed, the wound still raw and burning. Each gunshot drove into him like an accusation.

He tried to push himself up. His arms trembled, his chest heaved, and pain seared through him until his vision went dark at the edges. He collapsed back onto the bed with a growl.

From the doorway, Widow Hensley clucked her tongue. "You'll tear yourself open."

"I should be out there," Cole rasped. His jaw clenched, sweat running down his temple. "While they're marchin 'like sheep, Crowe's sharpin 'his knife. They'll never hold."

"Not with that attitude they won't," came Maggie's voice. She entered, wiping her hands on her apron, hair loose from the evening wind. "They're rough. They're scared. But they're standin', Cole. And standin 'is more than most in this town ever dared before."

Cole turned his face toward her, eyes fierce. "And what good am I, flat on my belly? What good's a man who can't lift a rifle?"

Maggie stepped close, leaning over him, her face inches from his. "You lit the spark, Hardin. Don't you forget it. You showed them Crowe could bleed. That's worth more than you know."

Cole's throat worked. He wanted to believe her. But the echo of the gunshots outside only deepened the ache in his chest.

Maggie set her hand firm on his shoulder. "Heal fast. They'll need you yet. But till then, you leave the fight to us."

Cole closed his eyes, fury and helplessness warring in his chest. Outside, the militia stumbled through their drills. Ragtag. Unready. But for the first time, willing to stand.

And Crowe would hear about it soon enough.

* * *

Cole sat on the edge of the narrow bed and let his fingers find the leather. The gunbelt felt foreign at first — heavy, awkward after days of lying flat — and the sight of his Colt made his ribs ache. Bandage edges peeked out where shirt had been cut away; the scar across his back stung like a fresh lash every time he twisted. He tasted iron and grit, but when he buckled the belt the world clicked into a shape he recognized. He was a man again, not a patient.

Maggie stood by the window with the curtain half-drawn, light cutting a strip across the floor. She watched him without pity. Jesse's absence had carved a new hardness into her face; tonight, that hardness softened only at the edges when she looked at Cole.

Tom Harper — wide-shouldered, grease still under his nails from the smithy — leaned in the doorway, shotgun in hand though his knuckles were white from something like fear and resolve together. Reverend Ezra Holt, his sleeves rolled and his jaw set, paced like a captain checking sails.

"You sure about this?" Tom asked. He wasn't asking whether the plan could work. He was asking if Cole was sure he could make it through.

Cole closed his eyes a second, feeling the world tilt as the bandage rubbed. "I don't get to be sure. I get to try. " He pushed to his feet, slow and deliberate, letting the pain ground him. "If we go soft now, Crowe'll come at us harder. Jesse's not bait — he's family. We go tonight."

Maggie stepped forward and checked the holster, watching him with the same blunt, practical tenderness she used on a sick horse. "You push yourself, you pass out in the middle of a raid and we drag you back like a dead mule. We don't do that. You ride smart, Hardin."

He nodded. A small, stubborn smile. "Smart's my middle name these days. Mostly by accident."

They gathered at the back of the church where the militia had assembled under Holt's direction. Lanterns burned low, casting faces into harsh geography: Eben Tate's weathered jaw, Mary Lou's hands clenched on the lantern pole, the blacksmith's knuckles scarred and sure. A handful more — a wagoner, a pair of brothers who'd shown up with rifles, the schoolteacher with a shotgun he'd borrowed from his uncle — clustered like a poor man's army. Not many. Not enough by numbers. Enough by will.

Holt spread a crude map on a wooden crate. He'd walked the ridges in daylight with Maggie; he knew the gulch where Crowe's camp lay, the scrubby cottonwoods that hid the outlaws 'fire, the single wash that supplied their horses. The plan was simple because they had to be: clean, sharp, with no room for heroics.

"First," Holt said, "this is a strike team — small and fast. Crowe's men outnumber us in open fight. We don't meet him there. We go at night, take advantage of the dark and their looseness after a night of drink."

Cole pointed with a finger that trembled only a little. "I take four. Maggie takes three with me. Tom, you and Eben hold the horses back at the ridge. Reverend, you and Mary Lou make the diversion — set a small fire on the opposite side of camp and make a hullabaloo. Get them moving that way. While they're lookin 'at the smoke, we get in, hit the guard lines, cut their hobbles, free the horses, and find Jesse."

Maggie barked a laugh that was half-mirth, half-relief. "You want me to get drunk and scream like an idiot, Reverend?"

Holt's mouth twitched. "If that's what it takes."

Cole studied their faces. "We take Deke and two of the heavy hands near Crowe's tent first. If they're watching near the horses, that's trouble. We need the mounts. No mounts, no quick pullout." He tapped the map. "We cut the lines they tie 'em with, not the hobbles. A cut girth they'll notice quicker — loosen the hobbles and a horse can slip if startled. The men fall apart if the mounts go. Jesse's been watched, but not chained for long. He's not a prisoner in irons — he's baits. He'll be in a bedroll or tied light. We drag him and split."

Tom's eyes narrowed. "What about Avery's death? Those men'll be keyed to blood." He spat the thought. "If we scare 'em, they'll shoot first and ask questions later."

"Which is why we're quick," Cole said. "No long firefights. Hit the sentries — a clean headshot or a knife quiet. You know how to do that, Tom. We get Jesse. We burn their supplies. We make it hurt enough that Crowe can't just sit 'til the town turns soft again."

Reverend Holt nodded slowly. "We take the preacher's rifle — not to kill, but to frighten. If Crowe loses a few of his comforts, his men's loyalty frays faster. Crowe buys loyalty with fear and spoils. Take the spoils, you sniff out the loyalty. We take enough to make 'em wonder."

Eben, who handled guns like a man who'd made peace with their weight, grunted. "We need to know guard rotations. Jesse knows. Might be risky to ask him to talk — but if he can slip a word at a window, or a message carved on a post, that'll tell us when to move." He looked hard at Cole. "If you go in, you don't come back here alone. You come back with him."

Cole's fingers closed on the butt of his Colt. "I'll come back. Even if I crawl."

They broke into teams and picked tools: rope, knives, a coil of wire. Maggie tied a strip of red cloth to her arm — a sign for Cole's group — then gave Holt a look that left no room for argument. The reverend handed out spare cartridges and wrapped a bit of cloth around the muzzle of his rifle to muffle it if need be. The blacksmith loaded a small keg of pitch and cloth — intended for the diversion Holt planned, not outright arson but enough smoke and shouting to make the drunkards tumble from their sleep.

The weight of the plan settled on them like a second skin. None of them fancied themselves soldiers. They'd never been more than townsfolk pressed into a shape by necessity. But their faces were set, and when Cole looked out at them he felt that old stubborn thread stitching him to life: he had started this. He would finish it.

Maggie stepped close, hand on his arm, thumb pressing through leather to bone. "You watch your back, Hardin. Don't be a hero. Be a leader."

He managed a breath and a crooked nod.

They left in staggered pairs: Holt and Mary Lou to the opposite ridge with the pitch, Tom and Eben to the horse line, Cole and Maggie with three others slipping low into the cottonwoods toward the gulch. Reverend Holt's prayer — short, sharp, more a benediction than supplication — fell out under his breath as they moved.

The night swallowed them like a promise.

Cole's boots sank into softer soil as they approached the camp. The world narrowed to the scrape of leaves, the slap of his own breath, the dull roar of a distant dog. Bandage rubbed, scar burned, gunbelt steady at his hips. He had a plan, and six ragged people who would die sooner than surrender their home. He had Maggie's hand at his back, steady as a bridle.

And somewhere in the dark, Crowe's men slept drunk, trusting in the fear they'd sown. They'd wake to something else entirely.

CHAPTER SEVENTEEN:
The Raid on the Hills

The militia moved like shadows through the cottonwoods, lanterns doused, rifles clutched in nervous hands. The night was cool, the ground soft underfoot, and every creak of saddle leather sounded like thunder in Cole's ears. His back burned, the scar pulling with each breath, but the weight of his Colt at his side steadied him.

Ahead, the orange glow of Crowe's fire bled through the trees. The outlaws 'laughter carried, rough and careless — they were drinking again. Cole motioned low, his hand flat, and the ragged line of townsfolk crouched in the brush.

Reverend Holt peeled off with Mary Lou and two others, dragging the pitch keg toward the far ridge. Within minutes, the faint flicker of flame rose against the dark. Shouts rang from camp — men scrambling, some grabbing rifles, others stumbling half-drunk toward the smoke.

"Now," Cole hissed.

The militia surged from the trees. Gunfire cracked, a ragged volley that shattered the night. Horses screamed, rearing as ropes were cut. Cole was already moving, pistol barking in his hand. A sentry dropped near the fire, another staggered with a cry.

Maggie was at his side, broom traded for a borrowed rifle. She fired once, the shot wild, then drove the butt hard into an outlaw's jaw when he rushed her. He hit the dirt, teeth scattering.

Jesse heard the chaos before he saw it. Bound near the water line, he jerked upright as the camp exploded in shouts and gunfire. His heart leapt — they'd come. He tore at the knots on his wrists, rawhide biting his skin. Then the frayed edge he'd worked nights on finally gave. His hands snapped free.

Smoke choked the gulch. Shadows darted, muzzle flashes lighting faces twisted with rage. Jesse ducked low, crawling past the fire, heart hammering. A drunken outlaw swung for him — Jesse grabbed a burning stick and rammed it into the man's gut. The outlaw screamed, stumbling back, giving Jesse the space to bolt.

"Cole!" Jesse shouted hoarsely.

Cole turned, saw the boy darting through the smoke. Relief surged like a flood. "Get to Maggie!" he roared, firing past Jesse's shoulder, dropping a man who'd raised his rifle at the boy's back.

The fight raged hot. The blacksmith swung his hammer into a rider's knee, sending him down screaming. Reverend Holt fired steady, voice carrying above the din: "Hold the line! Push 'em back!"

Crowe appeared at last, black hat low, rifle spitting fire. He moved through the smoke like a devil, his shot catching Eben Tate in the thigh, spinning him down. Crowe's men rallied around him, cursing, firing blind into the trees.

"Fall back!" one outlaw bellowed. "They've got more than we thought!"

The line broke. Crowe cursed, fury twisting his face, but even he couldn't hold them. The gang scattered, some fleeing with horses, others stumbling bloodied into the brush.

Cole dragged Jesse close, one hand gripping the boy's shoulder tight. Jesse's face was streaked with soot and fear, but his eyes burned with fire. "I told you I'd get free," Jesse gasped.

Cole almost laughed — almost — before pain pulled him sharp. "Good boy. Now stay close."

But Crowe wasn't finished. He stood at the edge of the firelight, smoke curling around him, eyes cold as steel. He raised his rifle once more, not to fire but to point at the town.

"You think this is over?" he shouted, voice cutting through the chaos. "Copper Creek's mine. I'll burn it to the ground before I let you take it."

Then he vanished into the dark, his oath hanging in the smoke like a curse.

The militia stood ragged in the wreckage, panting, bleeding, their rifles shaking in tired hands. But Jesse was free. And Crowe was not done.

* * *

They rode slow through the gray before dawn, the glow of the campfire they'd left behind still faint on the horizon. The horses were skittish, breath steaming in the cool air, their riders little better — bandaged, bloody, and bone-tired. The victory felt hollow in their bones.

Cole swayed in the saddle, pale under his hat, one hand pressed against his ribs where the scar pulled with every step of the horse. His eyes never left the boy riding beside Maggie.

Jesse sat stiff, soot streaking his face, hair singed at the ends, but he rode tall. He'd refused to be lifted up behind anyone. His wrists were raw from the ropes, his eyes too old now for his years, but he was free. And every time his gaze flicked to Maggie, his jaw set harder.

Maggie herself rode silent, her hand never straying far from Jesse's arm. Relief burned in her eyes, but so did fury. She didn't cry, not now. Not with Crowe's words still echoing: *I'll burn it to the ground.*

Behind them, Reverend Holt leaned heavy on his shotgun, riding double with the blacksmith whose arm had been grazed. Eben Tate limped onto his horse, thigh bound tight, grimacing at every jolt. Mary Lou carried herself with pride, lantern pole across her lap like a banner. They were ragtag, but they were still standing.

When Copper Creek came into sight, folk poured into the street. Faces pale, voices hushed — first at the sight of Jesse, then at the sight of bloodied riders. Someone shouted Maggie's name. A woman pulled Jesse down from the saddle, pressing him against Maggie before anyone could blink. Maggie crushed him in her arms, her shoulders shaking once, hard, before she mastered herself again.

"They did it," a man whispered. "The boy's back."

But the cheer that rose was short-lived. The militia's wounds were plain, and Crowe's shadow lay over them still. Everyone had heard the vow — word spread fast as smoke.

Cole slid from his horse, stumbling as his knees buckled. Tom and Holt caught him, steadying him on either side. He gritted his teeth against the weakness, forcing himself upright, his gunbelt heavy on his hips. His voice rasped, but it carried.

"Crowe's still out there. He's hurt, but he ain't gone. He'll come for this town next. You'd better be ready."

A silence followed, thick as a storm cloud. The townsfolk looked from Cole to Reverend Holt to Maggie. Fear was in their eyes, but so was something harder now — the first trace of defiance.

Maggie laid a hand on Jesse's shoulder. "He won't find us bowed. Copper Creek stands."

The cheer was quieter this time, but stronger. Not relief, not yet — determination.

Cole staggered, but Jesse stepped in, catching his arm. "I've got you," the boy said fiercely. Cole looked at him, pride flashing through the pain.

Crowe was out there in the dark, gathering his fury. But in Copper Creek, the people were gathering something too.

And the fight wasn't done.

CHAPTER EIGHTEEN:
Crowe's Vow

Crowe's horse lathered as he pulled up in a rocky gulch ten miles out, the night sky paling into dawn. He slid from the saddle, jaw tight, every movement sharp with fury. Around him, his men trickled in — bloodied, scattered, a handful missing altogether.

The camp they'd thrown together was a sorry sight. A few bedrolls dumped in the dirt, a fire snapping weakly, men clutching wounds and whiskey bottles. One cursed as he tied a rag around his arm. Another sat slumped against a rock, his face pale from a crease of bullet across his scalp.

Crowe stalked among them like a wolf through sheep. His black coat was scorched, his hat brim torn from a stray shot, but his eyes burned hotter than the fire.

"You call that a fight?" he snarled, voice cutting the morning air. "You let a bunch of shopkeepers and Sunday folk run you off like strays?"

One of the younger outlaws muttered, "They fought harder than we thought—"

Crowe's boot lashed out, kicking him square in the chest. The man toppled back with a grunt. Crowe leaned over him, pistol drawn, the barrel cold against the outlaw's forehead.

"Say that again," Crowe hissed.

The man froze, eyes wide, breath shallow.

Crowe holstered the gun with a snap and straightened, turning to the rest. "They got lucky. That's all. A spark. And sparks die easy. We'll snuff it out."

The gang shifted uneasily. Some nodded, but others avoided his gaze. Crowe saw the cracks — the doubt worming in — and it only fed his rage.

"They think a preacher, a woman with a broom, and a half-dead gunman make an army? I'll show 'em what an army looks like." He jabbed a finger toward the horizon, toward Copper Creek. "We'll burn their church. We'll drag their preacher through the street. And when I'm done, there won't be a roof left standing. I'll salt the dirt so nothing grows."

He yanked a knife from his belt and drove it into a log, the blade quivering. "This town's gonna learn fear ain't a word. It's a fire. And I'm the one who sets it."

The men cheered, but the sound was uneven, some voices loud, others thin. Crowe heard it — and it ate at him. He turned back, teeth bared.

"Any man here thinkin' he's got doubts, best ride now. 'Cause when I go for Copper Creek, I'll gut every coward who flinches. You ride with me, you ride to the bone."

Silence. No one moved. The fear held them in place. Crowe smiled thin and cruel.

"That's better."

He sat by the fire, pulling a flask from his coat, his eyes never leaving the rising sun. Copper Creek had dared to resist. They'd taken Jesse back, spilled his men's blood.

So, he'd make an example of them. A lesson carved in ash and smoke.

And he'd start with Cole Hardin.

Crowe paced the ragged edge of the camp like a man studying a map only he could see. The men hunched about the coals watched him, some with raw eagerness, some with the pale look of men who'd swallowed too much of their boss's poison already. The morning light had burned off the last blue of dawn; by noon the plan was already heavy in the air between them.

"You listen good," Crowe said, voice slow and poisonous. He spat into the dirt and folded his arms. "They hit us hard last night because we drank and slept like fools. That don't happen again. This time we make a clean, honest sheet of Copper Creek."

He drew a stick through the dirt, scratching a crude shape of the town: the church, the store, the boarding house, the livery, Clancy's spread out where the corrals sat. The men leaned in because Crowe's finger demanded attention.

"Three nights from now, when the moon rides high, we move at vespers. They'll be set—mustered from practice. They'll be tired. They'll be watchin 'like cowards at their windows. We hit at the bell." He tapped the little church mark. "We take the bell-house first. If you pull that rope and ring it in the dark, you can make a town think an army's on its doorstep. We'll use that confusion."

Deke, all scar and muscle, grinned and spat. "You want the preacher hung, boss?"

"I want him humiliated," Crowe said, and his grin was a blade. "You hang him if anyone gets cute. You drag him down Main and let folks see him sweat. Make the reverend smell his fear. Make every pious fool know that there's a price for pickin 'fights."

He scraped another line with the stick. "Tom Harper's smith? He's heavy-handed. We burn the smithy and the store next—Caldwell's runnin 'the shop, ain't she? Maggie's pride sits there. Torch it, take the ledgers, take what coin's left. If you take the shop, you take the town's belly." He pointed to the boarding-house marker. "We take the boarding-house last — drag out the sick, show 'em we can take what you love and throw it in the dirt."

A hush fell. The cruelty made even the hard men shift in their boots.

Crowe's voice dropped to a low, businesslike rasp. "We cut the water—sap their courage before they can put a fire out. Two men go to the pump and the wash. Break the wheel, slit the bucket lines. No water means a fire grows like a beast. You cut the mounts loose where you can't catch 'em; you burn the livery. No horses, no running. No running, town's trapped."

He looked up, eyes cold as flint. "We don't do this sloppy. We do it fast. Rafe, you and Cal take the north side toward the pump. Quiet. No shooting unless you have to. If the sheriff tries to get in the way, take him quiet. Don't parade him—bring him as leverage. If he won't be quiet, you make an example."

Rafe, a lean man who'd been quiet until now, swallowed and nodded. Crowe put a hand on his shoulder like a benediction. "You want the pay? You want the plunder? This is how you get it. But hear me: loyalty pays in coin and terror pays in obedience. You show me you'll kill to my will, and you eat fine."

The men muttered. Some spat in agreement. A few did not.

Crowe's finger hovered over a dot that marked the road to Clancy's ranch. "You take his house—light a quick blaze there and ride back slow. Let them see flames on the ridge. That'll set teeth on edge faster than a hundred sermons." His jaw tightened with a raw pleasure. "And bring me Cole Hardin if you can. Dead's easy. Alive is better for the show. Drag him out; let the world see what happens to a man who thinks he can teach me manners."

He stepped back from the scratch-map and fixed the circle with an order that brooked no argument. "We split in three. Deke takes the strike team for the church and store—fast and mean. He'll take the torch team. Rafe and Calhoun take the water and the livery. Two of you take the roads and watch for riders. If anyone from Copper Creek tries to sally or a neighbor shows up, you cut 'em off. Keep the roads tight."

A murmur at the edges, and Crowe's hawk-like eyes caught the sound. He turned, his voice a low drum. "Any man here squealing about mercy, any man with a soft belly, rides out tonight. I give you that chance. But if you stay, you do as I say, and you don't flinch."

In the circle of faces, some crumpled at that command; a few hardened with anger and greed. Deke smiled, the kind of smile that showed teeth meant for tearing. Rafe did not smile. He chewed the inside of his cheek and glanced away, the first small crack Crowe had noticed earlier becoming a line.

"Three nights," Crowe repeated. "At the toll of the bell, the sermon for vespers. We move then and we burn. We take what's theirs and we make them watch each scrap of it go. You bring me defiance, I'll teach them fear. "

He tipped his hat, a mock courtesy, and the men dispersed—some to sharpen knives, some to check powder, some to drink until their courage rotted into recklessness.

Crowe lingered at the edge of the fire until the last of his men had drifted away. He sat then, pulling a flask to his lips, and watched as the gullies below Copper Creek dreamed themselves small and fragile. In the quiet he muttered, not to any ear but to himself, "Let them try to hold a bell against my hand. Let them try."

The promise hung there like the smell of smoke—thick and sure.

CHAPTER NINETEEN:
The Churchyard Reckoning

The boarding house door burst open with a crash like a thunderclap that rattled the windows. Six of Crowe's men stormed inside—boots thudding, spurs jangling, the smell of sweat, horse and whiskey.

Before Cole could straighten from his chair they pounced. A hard fist to the gut doubled him over. Another kicked the legs from under him so the chair shattered under the impact. He hit the floor hard enough that the room spun; someone's boot print scored the wood near his ear. They yanked his shoulders back and hauled his arms behind him.

"Easy now," one of them drawled. "Boss just wants to talk."

No kindness came. Hands closed on his collar and hauled. Fingers dug into his shirt, ripping at fabric with a greedy, efficient tug until seams gave and the last of the cotton tore free, exposing a chest already bruised and raw. Mrs. Willard screamed from the kitchen doorway but one glare from the men sent her scurrying back into the shadows.

Cole fought, blood at the corner of his mouth. The air tasted like iron. "Tell Crowe if he wants a word, he can walk hisself here."

A backhand silenced him and a gag thrust home with a brutal shove that stole his voice. He coughed, tried to bite at it; a rough hand clamped over his jaw and banged his head against the doorframe to silence him.

Two men hauled him up and pushed him through the door. They dragged him out into the sun, boots thudding on the porch, and hands never loosening their hold.

Outside the small white chapel, the men flung him against the patio supports. They yanked his arms wide while another looped coarse rope around his wrists, stretching them out until his shoulders burned. The rough hemp scraped his skin raw as they tied him fast to the posts, spread-eagle beneath the wooden crossbeam.

The morning light spilled slow over Copper Creek, turning the churchyard gold. Word spread before the sun had fully cleared the rooftops — *they've got Hardin tied up at the church.* People began to gather.

"Crowe says folks been forgettin 'who runs Copper Creek," Deke Slater sneered, tightening the knot until Cole winced. "He figures you'll help remind 'em."

Cole's chest heaved, blood trickling down his cheek. He could see the faces of the town: shock, pity, shame. Maggie's face was there, fierce and pale, Jesse clinging at her sleeve. Cole wanted to speak to them, to tell them not to bow to Crowe, but the gag turned his breath to a muffled sound. He hung, his body stretched to breaking.

The men laughed low and mean, their shadows long against the church wall.

By the time Crowe rode in, most of the town had gathered. Shopkeepers, ranch hands, even the preacher stood on the edge of the dusty street, silent and pale. Crowe swung down from his horse in his long black coat, his spurs cutting through the hush like a clock ticking toward judgment.

Cole was bound to the wooden posts, wrists bleeding where the rope bit deep. He lifted his head when Crowe stopped in front of him — eyes steady, jaw set.

"Mr. Hardin," Crowe said, voice calm as a sermon. "Seems you been stirrin 'up trouble where none was asked for."

Cole's breath came ragged.

Crowe chuckled softly, glancing at the watching crowd. He stepped closer, the tip of his boot nudging the dust at Cole's feet. "Truth is, this town runs on order. Mine. And you—" he jabbed a gloved finger against Cole's chest "—you went and forgot that."

He turned, addressing the people now. "See what happens when a man mistakes pride for sense. He thinks one loud voice can stand against law."

"Law?" the blacksmith shouted. "You mean fear."

Crowe's smile faltered for a breath, then returned sharp as a knife. "Call it what you will. But by sundown, everyone here'll remember which it is keeps 'em safe."

He looked to his men. "Leave him. No water. Let the good folks ponder what defiance buys. I'll give you two days."

Crowe stood a step back in the doorway, the sun slanting off his hat brim so his eyes were little black coins. He watched Cole hang there like a wrong sermon nailed to the post, and the look on his face was all the satisfaction of a man who's just finished setting the terms of a deal he knows no one will accept.

He called out then—loud enough that windows rattled and heads poked from doorways. "Folks of Copper Creek!" His voice rolled down the street, smooth and practiced. "You've got two days. Bring me your dues by sunrise on the second day, or I'll hang him myself. No tricks. No sneakin 'off to save him. Two days. Decide what you love more: the man or your town."

Murmurs rippled through the watching crowd. Faces that had been white with fear the day before were paler still; some knuckled at their mouths, others stared at the dirt as if it might give an answer. Crowe let the silence sit on them a beat, then smiled thinly at the effect.

"We'll be watchin'," he added, and his men moved like a tide to take positions. They fanned out along Main Street, under windows, by the livery, along the alleys— hands on holsters, rifles cradled, eyes like hawks. Two men posted on the little hill behind the church, another pair took the shadowed lane by Maggie's store, and a pair stayed right at the boarding house where Cole had been taken from. Crowe left nothing to chance; their lines were tight and mean.

"You try anything," he said, addressing no one and everyone, "and I won't wait. I'll do it right then and there." He let the threat hang in the air, tasting of leather and tobacco.

Maggie stepped forward, jaw clenched so tight the knuckles whitened at her apron strings, but no one else moved with her. Old Nate's shoulders hunched as if to step, then he stayed rooted like a man held by iron. The preacher crossed himself, lips moving in a prayer that didn't reach the ears of Crowe's men.

As the riders settled and the town watched, Crowe waved once—cruel courtesy—and walked among his men, checking knots, tightening saddles, making sure their vigil would be merciless. He made them promise— no one gets near the church; no one helps Hardin. He laughed once, low and satisfied, and strode away into the dust, leaving his men like a cordon of shadow.

The crowd parted as Crowe mounted up again. horse's hooves echoing down the street.

Dust swirled around Cole's feet, his arms still stretched wide beneath the church cross — a living warning. But in his eyes, there was no surrender, only the slow, cold promise of payback.

* * *

The night crept in slow and heavy over Copper Creek, the kind of night where the stars shimmered like

195

cold coins in a black sky. The churchyard, which hours before was filled with gasps and stifled sobs, had gone still—except for the quiet shifting of the sentries Crowe had left behind.

Patrols circled like clockwork. Lanterns bobbed at the corners, voices were clipped and watchful. Crowe's men took turns on the posts; they spoke in short sentences, cursed at the moon, and kept their rifles close. The town slept in fits and starts behind shuttered windows, every creak magnified, every footstep a potential betrayal.

And up on the church posts, Cole hung—shirt gone, mouth bound, wrists chafed raw—eyes burning. He watched them watch the town, and in the jail of rope and wood he counted the hours, counting down toward whatever would come with the rising of that second sun.

Cole hung slumped against the beam and his skin was hot with fever and pain. If his head dropped in rest they kicked him awake. His lips were cracked, tongue swollen, but Crowe's men hadn't let a drop of water near him.

"Boss says he ain't to drink," one of them had said, leaning against the church steps with a lazy confidence. "Best he feels every hour of his choice."

Still—even in the cruelty, there were people who came.

Maggie arrived first, wrapped in a shawl with a lantern swinging from her hand. She didn't try to get close. The men had made it clear—anyone caught trying to help would get strung up right beside Cole. So, she sat instead on the bottom step of the church, near enough that he could see her if he lifted his head.

"I'm here, Cole," she whispered, soft enough the men at the corner wouldn't hear. "You ain't alone—not even now."

Old Nate came later, carrying a blanket he couldn't use. He laid it out in the dirt by the edge of the yard and sat on it with a groan, hat tipped low. He didn't speak a word, but his presence was solid—a wall against the dark.

"Lord help us," Maggie breathed when she saw him. "They near killed him."

"Not yet they haven't," Nate said, and moved forward.

Others came, too. A few ranch hands who owed Cole a kindness. A young mother who stood for half an hour before whispering a prayer and slipping away again. Even the preacher, who set a little candle in the dust and bowed his head.

"Lord have mercy," the preacher murmured. "Do not let this man bear his suffering unseen."

The guards scoffed. "Enough with that," one said, kicking dirt over the flame. "Crowe don't care for prayers."

Still, the people stayed.

Cole stirred once, head lifting just enough to scan the faces hovering between lamplight and shadow. He couldn't speak past the gag or free his arms, but his eyes found Maggie. For a moment—just a moment—his gaze softened, and she nodded back, chin trembling.

"I'll find a way," she promised under her breath. "You just stay alive."

The men on watch—lean shadows with rifles slung across their shoulders—shifted uneasily as the quite thickened. One of them spat and eyed the folks sitting in the dark.

"Fools," he said. "He's a dead man walkin'. What good's all this loyalty gonna do?"

But Cole Hardin wasn't dead. Not yet. And for every hour Copper Creek stayed sitting in that dirt, watching with him, something in the town's spine began to straighten. The silence wasn't fear anymore—it was waiting.

And when the morning came, it would come with a choice. And this time, Copper Creek might not look away.

Cole lifted his head. Sweat and blood streaked his face, but his eyes still burned with defiance.

Maggie, pale and sleepless, rose from the bottom step of the church and brushed the dust from her skirts. Her eyes were tired but fierce. She moved closer without stepping over the invisible line Crowe's men guarded.

"You held on," she whispered. "You did it."

Old Nate leaned forward from his place on the blanket, squinting up at Cole. "Damn right he did," he grunted. "Stronger than any ten of us." His voice cracked. "Still ain't right, leavin 'him that way."

One of Crowe's men—young, smooth-faced, more uncertain than the rest—glanced between the group and Cole's trembling frame. "You should leave," he muttered. "Boss ain't gonna like what he sees if you stay here."

Maggie didn't budge. She looked at the guard with a steady, breaking calm. "Then let him not like it," she said. "We've done enough cowering."

The words hung in the cool dawn—so simple, yet they shifted everything. People from the boarding house stood in doorways. The blacksmith crossed his arms and watched. Young Jesse, standing now by the livery fence, met Maggie's gaze and gave a small, certain nod.

It was the first crack in Crowe's wall.

Footsteps echoed down the street. A figure approached—the preacher, walking tall with his Bible tucked under his arm. His voice rang out clear in the quiet morning.

"I will not leave a man to suffer without witness," he said. "Nor will I deny him water while breath still fills his body."

And there it was. A choice made aloud. A challenge drawn in the dust of dawn.

The guards stepped forward—hands twitching near their guns—but something was changing. There were more townsfolk now than there were guns. And the town, long bruised and cowed, had begun to stand up.

The preacher stepped past the invisible line. Nate stood beside him. Maggie took a stride forward, jaw high and steady. One by one, people moved into place—not with weapons, but with courage.

"Get back," the head guard snapped, rifle rising. "Ain't nobody touchin 'Hardin—orders is orders."

For the first time, Maggie didn't stop. Her voice was clear, cool, deadly quiet. "Then you're gonna have to shoot us first."

The guard hesitated. His rifle wavered. Behind him, the others looked around—uncertain, outnumbered, shaken by the quiet resolve of people who had run out of surrender.

And in the pale light of morning, with Cole Hardin still bound but not broken, Copper Creek took its first breath of freedom.

The moment was suspended, waiting. And Crowe didn't know it yet…

…but the fear was starting to slip out of his fingers.

* * *

The news reached Crowe at mid-morning, carried by a breathless rider with too much dust on his jacket and too much fear in his eyes.

Crowe was seated outside the clapboard saloon at Bitter Creek Junction—three miles down the rail line, where he and his men had been waiting to hear how the night went. He didn't look up at first, just kept pouring whiskey into a tin cup, casual as a man sitting on his porch. But when the rider stammered the words—

They're standin with him, Crowe. Town's… all around the church. They ain t moving."—something sharp flickered across Crowe's face.

The tin cup paused halfway to his lips.

"They're doin 'what?" he asked quietly.

The rider swallowed. "They... they stayed with him. Preacher. Maggie Harlan. Nate. More folks than not. They're standin 'up to the boys you left on watch."

Crowe set the cup down without drinking. Slowly. Carefully. The sun beat hard on the dusty street, but the temperature shifted—flat-out dropped—as Crowe rose from his chair.

"Did they cut him down?" he asked.

"N-not yet. But they're—"

"They're what?" Crowe snapped, voice as sharp as a fang. "Waiting? Comforting? Whispering hope into a dead man's ear?"

The rider opened his mouth, then seemed to think better of speaking.

Crowe didn't wait for more. He strode toward his horse, movements clipped and precise—a man coiled to strike. His lieutenants stood up, rifles half-lifted, faces already tightening at the message they sensed behind his silence.

"Mount up," Crowe ordered. "Full ride. We end this now."

"But boss—" one of them stammered, "town'll be waitin'."

"Then make sure they regret it." Crowe swung into the saddle, eyes fixed on Copper Creek as if he could already see it burning. "They think defiance buys 'em mercy. We'll show 'em the real price."

He yanked the reins and snapped a command. The horses leapt forward in a storm of dust and pounding hooves, the gang riding like a black river into the rising heat of the day.

By the time the first rooftops of Copper Creek came into view, every man riding behind Crowe could feel the warpath in him—like a wildfire waiting on a match. He meant to crush the town's spirit, scorch their courage until nothing remained but ash and apology. He meant to make them watch as Cole Hardin fell for good.

And in the shadow of the churchyard, where Maggie and Old Nate and the preacher stood like stubborn stone against the wind, something in the air shifted. The sound of hooves—rushing, relentless—rose like thunder.

Maggie turned her head. The color drained from her face. "He's here."

The war wasn't coming anymore. It was on their doorstep.

* * *

The sun had climbed a little higher when the sound of hooves returned — slow, deliberate. Crowe rode in again, coat flaring behind him like a dark banner. The crowd that had lingered near the church fell silent. Only the creak of saddle leather and the whisper of dust marked his coming.

Crowe dismounted without a word. In his hand gleamed a coiled whip — black, braided, and hungry for use. He let it unroll in the dust with a hiss that made the nearest bystanders flinch.

Crowe stepped forward with the calm of a man arranging a stage. "There," he said, voice carrying. "That's how you break a man. Not flat in the dirt where he can hide his face. High and bare, where all of you can see. Reckon talk alone won't teach you," Crowe said quietly. "Maybe this will. Watch close, now. Learn your lesson."

A couple of his men hauled Cole forward a notch so the beam put his chest and back well in view of the crowd. The gag stifled his sound. Cole's ribs rose and fell fast; his shoulders trembled where the rope bit in. He looked at Crowe with something like hunger—less for mercy than for the moment when this would end.

Crowe lifted the whip. –The first lash came sudden and sharp, leather snapping across his back. Fire lit every nerve, the stretch of his arms making the pain worse. His boots jerked off the boards, a half-groan caught under the gag. The second blow tore his breath short; the third buckled his knees, but the ropes dragged him upright again. The next last struck with a sharp flare of pain that made his shoulders hitch and his body arch. The crowd sucked in breath as though the wind had been knocked out of them.

Again and again Crowe struck. The lashes were deliberate, each one finding the same track so the pattern bloomed across skin—red, then darker, an ugly map of punishment. Cole rocked with every blow, wrists straining at the knots. He tried to turn his face away; his jaw worked around the gag. Sweat, blood, dust—life and violence—matted his hair to his forehead.

The people watched as if they'd come to see a lesson delivered. Some couldn't look—eyes clamped shut behind trembling fingers. Others stared, faces hardening into an ugly, guilty fascination. Maggie stood at the edge of the crowd, white of cheek and furious, fingers curled on the bonnet string until her knuckles showed. Old Nate's lips pressed into a thin line; Jesse's hands shook visibly at his sides.

Crowe's face never changed. He cracked the whip again, a sharp arc that bit across Cole's exposed shoulder. Cole jerked, then steadied, the set of his jaw telling the town what his screams would have said. The gag kept the sound out; the motion of his head— swallowing, eyes blazing—did the rest.

The crowd flinched with every strike. Mothers pulled children away from windows, men clenched fists but did not move. Some wept. Some cursed. And Crowe walked slow circles around his prize, savoring every sound.

"You think Copper Creek has a backbone?" Crowe asked, his grin sharp as a spur. "Look here. This is what your courage looks like. A man strung up and begging without words."

Cole's vision blurred, but he forced his jaw shut, forced himself not to cry out. He thought of Maggie's eyes, Jesse's stubborn chin. He let the pain become rhythm, each lash a step counted, each groan a mark on a ledger he swore to balance. Cole's body arched against the ropes, but he bit back the cry that wanted to escape.

Again. And again. Each strike landed with cruel precision, the leather singing, the crowd shrinking back in horror. Mrs. Willard turned away, covering her mouth. Old Nate clenched his fists but didn't move; even the preacher's lips trembled, whispering a prayer under his breath.

Crowe stepped closer, breath coming heavy now, eyes bright with something malicious. "This is what happens to men who forget their place," he said. "This is what keeps Copper Creek quiet."

Then, without warning, he struck once more — harder than before — before letting the whip fall to his side.

Crowe's words hung in the air like smoke that wouldn't clear.

Cole's body throbbed beneath the rope, every heartbeat a reminder of his own weight hanging against the post. Sweat trickled down his temples. The gag bit into the corners of his mouth. He could feel the rope grinding against raw skin each time he breathed.

But his eyes stayed open.

And that burned Crowe worse than the silence ever could.

The preacher's hands trembled, but they didn't rise. His voice shook as it slipped out, hoarse and full of something like prayer. "Mercy is not weakness," Holt said. "Cruelty is not power."

Crowe didn't even look at him. "I told you to preach inside the church, Holt," he said, voice cold as rusted iron. "You open your mouth again out here, I take more than your words."

Holt's jaw tightened — but he stayed silent.

He looked at Cole instead. And something in his eyes said: *I'm here. I see you. Hold on.*

When Crowe paused, the hush that followed was thick and full of what they'd all seen. He let them have that stillness. Then, in the slow, cold way of a man savoring power, he waved the whip, the leather folding softly back into his hand.

They denied Cole water, dangled a cup before his lips then snatched it back. When he swayed close to fainting, a boot to his ribs snapped him awake again. Humiliation became the point, cruelty the currency. Crowe wanted the town to see its would-be hero reduced to a bleeding, sweating husk.

When Sheriff Silas Boone stepped forward at last, voice shaking but loud, Crowe only laughed. Boone stood between Cole and Crowe, badge gleaming dull in the lamplight. "No more," Boone said. "You don't take more."

The shot that dropped him came sudden, merciless. Boone pitched into the dust. Silence swallowed the square. Maggie screamed and fought to reach him, Jesse clinging to her arm, but the rifles kept her back.

Cole groaned behind the gag, the sound torn from his chest like a sob. His body burned, arms near numb, but the sight of Boone's body lit a different kind of fire inside him. Rage cut through the pain. He would not let Boone's sacrifice be wasted.

Maggie was farther back — held in place by a wall of church steps and half the town's fear. Her fists were closed so tight her nails dug into her palms. Wet tracks burned down her cheeks, but she didn't sob. Didn't beg.

She watched.

She memorized.

Every lash. Every word. Every breath.

Jesse stood in front of her — too young, too angry, hands balled into fists he didn't know how to use.

Crowe rode that silence. Let it fester.

He paced in front of Cole, boots dragging dust in slow circles, voice low and sharp.

"That's your problem, Hardin. Thinkin 'a man's worth somethin 'just because he don't back down. Like your silence is some kind of shield." He leaned in, lips near Cole's ear. "A quiet man dies same as a screamin ' man. The rope don't care."

Cole's breath hitched. His shoulders burned. His vision blurred at the edges. But the fire in his eyes stayed.

He *would not* give Crowe the satisfaction.

Not a sound. Not a plea.

Just defiance — raw, wordless, and alive.

Inside his own skull, beneath the gag, pain and memory twisted together like torn threads:

Heat pressed into his back, the sting of the whip, the rope eating through raw skin.

Her voice—Maggie's—echoing from somewhere he couldn't see.

Jesse's smaller silhouette, fists trembling like gun barrels about to burst.

Boone on the ground.

The town—silent, broken—watching.

Pain.

Fury.

Hold. Don't bow. Don't let him win.

Cole blinked once. Slow. Intentional.

He held Crowe's stare.

Crowe saw it. And the smile dropped from his face.

"What you think you got there?" Crowe asked him. "Pride? Willpower?" He placed a hand on Cole's chest, just below the throat. "All I see is a man too stubborn to understand he already lost."

Crowe stepped back, making a grand gesture to the crowd.

"This is what happens," he said, raising his voice to the whole square. "You want to see where pride gets you? Look right here. Look closely. A man who won't kneel—dies where he stands."

The gang laughed behind him. A few townsfolk flinched. But one or two didn't.

One of them was Maggie.

She let one more tear fall — then wiped the rest away with the back of her hand. "Then we'll build him back up," she whispered.

And the spark landed. Somewhere inside Cole Hardin's agony, it caught light.

Crowe raised his hand. He spoke to the town like a judge delivering sentence. "Tomorrow," he said. "Tomorrow bring me what I want—coin, cattle, tribute—or I burn your homes and hang your hero here where he dangles now."

The crowd broke—some rushing forward with coins, others fleeing into houses, still others stiffening with fury. Maggie's voice cut through, raw and hoarse. "You hear me, Copper Creek! You let him take one more thing and he owns you all!" Her words cracked, but steel lay under them.

Cole hung there, body broken open by pain, half-conscious, the look in his eyes — what little strength still burned there — was enough to tell every soul watching that Crowe hadn't broken him. Not yet.

His back throbbed, wrists raw, lungs aching, but he clung to one thought: *They made me their lesson. I'll make them regret it.*

They left him like that, ropes coiled, boots scraping the earth as they melted away down the street, their shadows long and slow over the church boards. Cole sagged against the strain but did not yield; his jaw worked around the gag, and though the sound was muzzled there was a promise in the set of his shoulders: this was not done.

Cole swayed where he hung, chest rising and falling in shallow, stuttering breaths, every one a reminder of the lashes across his back and shoulders. They burned and throbbed, his skin hot with fever and pain. But beneath the pain something like fury smoldered. He lifted his head and met the eyes of the town—those who'd watched and those who'd looked away—and in that look was a question that hadn't yet gone quiet: what will you do with what you've seen?

They'd left Copper Creek in smoke and silence, the people's courage whipped out of them along with Hardin's strength.

Now Crowe sat at his fire, whiskey bottle in hand, boots stretched toward the flames. His men circled like carrion birds, drunk on the memory of what they'd done.

Deke was loudest, acting it out, whipping at the night air with a belt, laughing. "You should've seen him! Strung up high on that church post, arms pulled like a scarecrow. Man couldn't even keep his boots under him." He mimed Cole's knees buckling, grinning wide.

The others howled with laughter. "Hardin, the big hero!" Calhoun jeered. "Looked more like a sack of wheat dangling there."

Crowe let them have their noise a while. He liked to hear them spit their versions — every story proved the lesson had landed. But when he finally stood, the fire dropped into silence.

"You saw it," he said, low and steady. "You saw what happens when a town thinks it can rise. Hardin stretched on that post like a trophy. That's how you choke the fight out of people."

He kicked a log into sparks. "But don't think it ends there. The whipping, the coins, the tears — that's just the start. Fear fades if you let it. So we burn deeper. We torch their barns, bleed their cattle, starve their bellies."

His men shifted closer, the glow of fire painting their faces eager.

"Tomorrow," Crowe went on. "That's their mercy. Tomorrow to bring me what I want. And if they don't, I hang Hardin until he don't breathe. And the whole damn town will watch him swing."

A murmur of approval rolled through the gang — laughter, curses, the hungry clatter of men savoring cruelty. Crowe drank deep from the bottle, felt the burn, and smiled.

He believed the town was his already

CHAPTER TWENTY:
The Noose Tightens

He had given the town until tomorrow. Crowe's ultimatum had hung in the air like a threat you could measure by the hour — bring all their dues or watch Copper Creek burn. People moved like ghosts, windows shuttered, children kept close, prayers hasty and whispered.

On the morning of the second day the town gathered in the square because Crowe wanted them there. Gunmen ringed the edges of Main Street, rifles angled down at the dirt, but eyes sharp as razors.

Cole was still tied to the church post — bruised, blood at the corners of his mouth, the lash wounds on his back stark ridges of red and purple.

Cole stirred as the sun warmed his bruised skin. His throat was like sand and fire, but the sight of faces still gathered beneath him lent him something that hadn't been broken—something that felt like hope.

Crowe sat the whole time, calm in the shade, chewing on the end of a cigar. He gestured lazily toward the lumber already stacked near the boardwalk. The posts, the crossbeam, the rope coiled like a snake. All waiting.

"You'll build it," he said to the crowd, voice loud but casual. "You'll dig the hole, raise the beam, lash the rope.

You'll put up the gallows that'll hang the man who made you think you were safe."

No one moved.

Not at first.

Eben took one step and stopped, jaw working. Widow Hensley shook her head. One of the Callahan boys put his hand to his mouth and turned away. Someone retched behind the mercantile.

Crowe let the silence stretch.

Then he fired one shot into the street — right between Maggie Caldwell's feet.

"I said build it," he growled.

Eben stepped forward. Hands shaking. Voice flat. "Don't give me a choice, do you?"

Crowe pointed with his gun. "You got all the choice you want, Eben. You help build it… or you climb it."

They brought shovels. They dug the holes. They lifted the timber, shoulders straining under the weight of it. They nailed braces, hammered pegs, tied knots.

They built the instrument of death they were meant to witness.
And Cole watched — teeth clenched beneath the gag, fury mixed with fear biting deeper than any rope ever could.

They wouldn't look at him.

Even though Cole was tied just twenty feet away —
arms bound high to the church post, sweat and blood
drying on his skin in the rising sun — most of the people
lifting the boards, digging the holes, tying the knots
couldn't meet his eyes.

He couldn't speak through the gag Crowe had
forced on him. He couldn't move his arms or turn his
head. All he could do was watch.

And what he saw cut deeper than the ropes
burning through his wrists.

He saw Eben Talbot, the blacksmith, shoulders
heaving beneath the weight of the crossbeam. The man's
strength wasn't in doubt. But his hands shook. The same
hands that once reshaped iron with fire and force now
trembled under the burden of wood meant for death. Now
he helped build a scaffold.

He saw boys — no older than Jesse — staring at
the construction with hollow eyes. Some were old enough
to carry hammers. Most weren't old enough to
understand what it meant to be broken into obedience.

And he saw the mothers.

Arms around their children. Holding them back.
Holding them still. Holding them in place because
resistance wasn't just dangerous — it was fatal. Some
cried openly. Some cried without tears. Some stared at
the boards, hands over mouths, trying not to breathe a
thing that felt like surrender.

Every breath hurt Cole — not from his wounds, but from the truth settled heavy in his chest:

Crowe didn't just want him dead.
He wanted them all to break themselves to do it.

The sound of the hammer echoed like artillery.
Every strike was a confession.
I want to live.
I don't dare refuse.
I don't know how to stop this.

Eben drove in the pegs one by one — each strike slower than the last.

"God forgive us," someone whispered.

"Don't say that out loud," another hissed. "You'll bring them down on us."

Two women hurried children back inside the boarding house, covering their ears.

But the children still saw.
They saw their fathers build death for a man who tried to save them.
They saw their mothers too afraid to interfere.

A little girl with a torn ribbon in her hair turned away from the gallows-in-progress and looked at Cole. Just looked. No fear. Just confusion — like she couldn't understand how a man who looked so tired and hurt could deserve this.

Cole forced himself to stand taller. If he was going to die today, he wasn't going to let the last thing that girl saw be surrender.

Crowe leaned back in his saddle, watching them all.

Hands behind his head.
Boots hooked in the stirrups.
Smile like he'd invented victory.

"This is what order looks like," he said to no one and everyone. "Man does what he's told and lives. Man decides he's bigger than that?" He gestured toward Cole with the tip of his cigar. "He hangs where everybody can learn the lesson."

The gang chuckled.

Maggie didn't move.

She stood in the church doorway, fists balled at her sides. She didn't join the work. Didn't turn away, either. Just stared — as if memorizing every nail, every board, every word Crowe uttered — storing it all like kindling for the day she got to burn him down.

Jesse stood beside her, knuckles white around the rifle he wasn't allowed to raise. He watched Cole. Never looked away.

Then the final pegs went in.
The beam was raised.
The rope was thrown over.

218

The gallows was complete.

And as the last hammer fell silent, something inside Copper Creek shifted.

Not in fear.

In anger.

Not loud.

But alive.

Cole felt it. Under the agony. Under the ropes. Under the silence they shoved down his throat.

He felt it.

And so, did Crowe.

That's why Cole smiled.

Because nothing scared a tyrant more than the moment a town remembered it was still a town.

The gallows stood finished in front of the church — stark against the sky, the rope swaying like a promise. The town held its breath.

A single man climbed the steps first — Rafe Donner, Crowe's executioner. He tested the platform, stomping twice. The hinges creaked with a cruel, clean sound.

"Solid," he said.

Crowe nodded from atop his horse. "Now drop the sandbag."

A heavy burlap sack was brought up — tied with the same rope height Crowe wanted for Cole. Rafe looped it, checked the knot, and kicked the lever.

THUD. The bag dropped through. The platform bounced, swung, then stilled.

Cole turned his head away, his heart hammering in his chest. Even bound to the post, he could feel the weight of that sound like it belonged to him.

They came for him then.

Calhoun and Mack Jenson cut the ropes that bound his arms to the church post. Cole collapsed to his knees, breath ragged. They hauled him upright, hands working too quick to be called careful. His wrists were tied behind his back. The gag still cut deep into his mouth.

He stood on his own for the first time in days — swaying, weak, but still refusing to bow.

Crowe watched, savoring every step toward the gallows. "Walk him," he said.

They pushed him up the stairs, his chest heaving, the gag muffling his rasp of breath.

The boards creaked. The rope hung above. Sunlight glinted off the knot.

They forced him to the center of the platform and tied his ankles. Rafe stood ready to kick the lever.

The crowd pressed in at the edges—faces blanched, hands at mouths, the hollow silence of people who'd been told how to be afraid. Even the preacher's fingers trembled on his Bible.

Crowe stepped forward. He ran the noose once through his hand as if testing the weight of the thing, then slipped it up beneath Cole's chin. The hemp smelled of tar; it felt final in the morning air.

"You ever think about beggin'?" Crowe asked, voice low, almost casual.

Cole's eyes burned and he shook his head slowly.

Crowe leaned in close, breath heavy with smoke and dust, eyes narrowed to slits.

"Never crossed your mind, did it?" he said, almost gently — like a man admiring a rare trait in a dying animal. "That's the kind of pride they write songs about. Men stand up for it… men die for it."

He paused, voice dropping to a cold whisper.

"But pride don't make you bulletproof, Hardin. Pride don't save nobody. You keep your chin up all you want — it just gives a cleaner shot when it's time to put you in the ground."

Crowe tilted his head, studying Cole the way a butcher might look over prime cattle before the cut. The gag was cinched tight between Cole's teeth, blood at the corners of his mouth, but his gaze stayed clear — steady, even now.

Crowe clicked his tongue.

"Look at you," he drawled. "Still starin 'me down like you think you're better than the rest of us. Like pain don't touch you."

He leaned in close, voice low and cold.

"You think pride makes you strong? You think grit keeps a man alive?"

He let the silence stretch a breath.

"Pride don't stop a rope from tightenin'," he said softly. "Ain't never saved a neck from breakin', neither."

Cole didn't flinch.

Crowe straightened, wiped the dust off his gloves, and smiled without warmth.

"Hangin 'don't care how tall you stand, Hardin," he murmured. "It just cares how long you fall."

The rope tightened around Cole's throat. It was rough hemp. Dry. Coarse. It dug into his skin before it even bore weight.

Crowe turned to the crowd.

"Here's your lesson, Copper Creek," he said, voice loud and lazy. "Here's what it costs to spit in the face of law. Here's what it costs to stand taller than you've earned."

Faces in the crowd crumpled — mothers, ranchers, children. Even Reverend Holt's jaw shook as he whispered prayers through clenched teeth.

No one moved.

Crowe turned to Cole, meeting his eyes.

"You look like a man who's still got somethin 'to say," he murmured, tapping the gag with one finger. "Shame no one gets to hear it."

Then he leaned in closer, dropping his voice to a whisper meant only for Cole.

"You shoulda begged. Men who beg get mercy. Men who don't…"
He straightened, letting the words hang. "Men like that get remembered. But they don't get saved."

Cole stared back at him — through the pain, through the heat, through the fading breath in his lungs. He didn't have words.

But he still had thought. *I'm not dyin 'for what I did. I'm dyin 'for what you're afraid I'll do. And that means you already lost.*

Crowe saw it — the glint of defiance, not pride, but purpose. And it chilled him more than a bullet.

He turned to the crowd. "You think him dyin 'is the tragedy? Him livin 'was worse. Because it gave you hope. And hope is what burns slow."

"STOP!!" someone yelled.

Crowe chuckled. "So that's it then. You aim to fight me over this boy?"

The preacher stepped forward first. "We aim to stand for what's right, Crowe," he said. "You won't get your hanging today."

A soft ripple ran through the crowd—fear, yes—but courage too.

Crowe's eyes narrowed. "And what do you think happens next, Reverend? You reckon I just ride on home? Count it as a fine debate?"

Jesse spoke up then, cracking voice steady as a struck match. "We reckon you go back the way you came—if you're smart enough to see what's changed."

Crowe stared. A slow smile cut across his face.

"We'll see." He gave the signal.

Rafe put his boot on the lever.

The crowd held breath.

Jesse screamed, "NO!—"

The platform dropped.

And Cole Hardin fell.

The rope caught.

Cole's body snapped downward, then jerked to a stop so violently that every joint screamed. His boots kicked, scraping air. For one terrible second Cole's feet hung free and the world narrowed to the pressure at his throat and the pounding behind his ears. His hands clawed uselessly at the rope, shoulders dragging against the strain. The sound that came out of him wasn't a scream—more a strangled groan muffled by the gag. The noose bit deep into his neck, crushing breath, turning the world red at the edges.

The sky flickered. The square blurred.

He heard his own heartbeat—loud, erratic, hammering inside his skull—and nothing else for a second. His vision tunneled; the edges went black.

Below him, the crowd erupted.

Women cried out. Men surged forward and were shoved back by gun barrels. Reverend Holt's voice broke in the chaos—"Cut him down! For God's sake, cut him down!"—before someone struck him across the mouth.

Jesse tried to run forward. Two of Crowe's men caught him, lifting him off the ground as he kicked and screamed, "Let him go! Let him go!"

Maggie fought her way through the crowd, wild-eyed, her hair coming loose. "Stop this! You bastards, stop it!" She shoved past Holt, shouldered her rifle and leveled it at the gallows. Her hands shook, but her voice didn't. "Drop that rope or I swear I'll—"

A single rifle crack splits the air. The bullet struck the crossbeam. Wood splintered.

The rope frayed—then snapped.—

CHAPTER TWENTY-ONE:
The Reckoning

Cole dropped like a stone, crashing to the ground in a tangle of limbs and dust. He hit hard, shoulders twisting, lungs convulsing as air tore back into them. The gag ripped loose when he gasped. He rolled once, half-conscious, coughing, retching, until blood spotted the dirt.

Crowe stood frozen, eyes narrowed into ice. "Seize them! Get him back up!" he barked, voice sharp.

"Get him!" Maggie shouted. "Move!"

Crowe's men surged to close ranks, but the line between them and the town had shifted. Where once there had been only fear, there was now motion—a dozen people stepping forward at once, something like courage stitched from whatever remained in their chests.

Then, with a hard, impatient curse, Crowe signaled his men. They closed on Cole again, but the crowd—no longer merely watching—moved, a living wedge between Cole and Crowe's men. It wasn't yet a disorderly retreat, and Crowe's pride still stood in his chest; the threat of worse kept him from full attack.

Cole lay there coughing, fingers white with effort. Around him, people staggered under the rush of what they'd just done: saved a man, perhaps invited a war. The choice Copper Creek had to make now wasn't whether they could be brave—they had been—but whether they would be brave together.

Reverend Holt and Eben were there first, cutting the knots at his wrists, pulling him away from the noose as more shots cracked from the edge of town.

Jesse dove to Cole's side, hand shaking as he poured water from his canteen over the raw welt around Cole's neck. "It's all right," he kept saying, voice breaking. "You're all right, Cole. You're all right."

Cole tried to speak, but the words rasped out thin. He pushed a hand against Jesse's arm instead—solid, wordless gratitude.

Then he looked up at the gallows, still swaying, empty rope ends fluttering in the wind. His throat burned, vision swimming, but one thought cut through everything else:

You're finished, Crowe.

He dragged in a breath that tasted of dust and fire.

And in that quiet, Cole's voice cracked—raw, but yelling something no one could miss. His body strained, desperate, pleading.

He wasn't begging for his life.

He was begging the town not to bow.

Crowe raised his hand to signal the charge.

Time froze.

And then—from the far end of the street—came another sound.

A shout.

Bootsteps.

A rifle being cocked that didn't belong to Crowe's men.

Several riders appeared in the distance—moving at a clipped speed, dust rising behind them. But these were not Crowe's. They came from the west. And they were armed.

One of them cupped his hands near his mouth as they slowed, calling out in a voice that carried like a crack of lightning:

"You got my friend tied up, Crowe? Or is this another of your charity shows?"

It was Clancy. And behind him? Three other ranchers, guns drawn, eyes alive with the look of men who'd finally made their choice.

Crowe turned—suddenly not so sure of the count anymore.

The town held its breath, waiting for the spark.

And one thing was now clear:

The tide had turned.

Crowe didn't back down. He didn't take a step, didn't blink. But the hint of surprise in his eyes was there—just a flicker—when Clancy and his riders drew closer, weapons raised.

"You're a bold fool, Clancy," Crowe called, voice carrying just fine over the graveside quiet. "You got three men with you. I've got nine. You can't win."

Clancy didn't hesitate. "Maybe not. But it ain't just us anymore." He nudged his horse forward, sweeping his eyes across the crowd. "Folks here are mighty tired of bowin 'to you. Seems like you're the only one who hasn't figured that out."

Crowe's lip curled. "They had their chance. Now they're gonna pay for takin 'his side." He nodded toward Cole, still glaring hate at the man who'd tried to break him.

"Boys," Crowe barked, "get ready. We'll make an example out of the whole damn lot."

That was the match.

Eben drew first. The young ranch hand's pistol flashed from his belt and boomed once—loud and raw. The bullet clipped the shoulder of the closest of Crowe's men. The man swore and ducked, but it was too late. The standoff shattered.

Gunfire exploded in all directions. Crowe's men turned toward the newcomers—and toward the townsfolk. Bullets tore splinters out of the church posts. Women screamed and dove behind barrels; Nate shoved Maggie down and drew the heavy colt he hadn't fired since the cavalry took his leg. The preacher knelt beside Cole even as shots rang past.

Clancy and his riders whipped their reins and charged, blasting fire from their revolvers. They might've looked outnumbered, but they weren't alone anymore.

Men from the livery jumped into the street with shotguns from behind loaded wagons. A ranch wife stepped out from beside Maggie's store, rifle braced against the doorjamb. Even Old Nate got off a round, knocking one of Crowe's gunhands off his saddle with a grimace and a muttered, "Still got it in me."

Crowe ducked behind his horse, firing controlled and vicious. His shots were perfect—calm in the chaos, like a man who'd lived half his life in a fight. He winged Clancy's arm and dropped a young stable boy who'd dared to fire wide and fast.

But in the chaos, the edge was shifting.

"Get up, son," Nate shouted over the thunder. "Ain't no fight you want to watch from the ground!"

Cole staggered, breath burning like fire, legs shaking. The preacher pressed a pistol into his hand without a word.

Cole looked toward Crowe. Eyes blazing. Jaw set.

The man had tried to break him. Tried to hang him. Tried to own him.

Cole raised the gun.

Gunfire punched the air, loud and ragged, echoing off the storefronts of Copper Creek like a storm trying to shake the town loose. Men shouted. Horses screamed. The dust rose so thick it might've been gun smoke alone. But through it all, Cole Hardin stood—fists bruised, back bleeding, rope burns raw across his neck and his wrists—and stared straight at Crowe.

Crowe was still firing from behind his horse, calm as a man firing at tin cans. He leveled his revolver, dropped another of Clancy's riders with a single round, then grabbed for more bullets from his belt.

That's when he saw Cole.

Standing.

Gun in hand.

Hatless. Gag torn off. Shirt gone. Scars and fury on full display.

Crowe's smug jaw went still. For just a heartbeat, his face flickered—not fear, not quite—but the ghost of something colder. Recognition.

"You should've stayed hangin', Hardin," he snarled.

Cole didn't answer. Didn't smile. Didn't blink.

He stepped forward through the chaos—through stray bullets and broken boards and ringing echoes—and Crowe stepped out to meet him.

The street went quiet in a way no gunfight ever should. A kind of hush fell—the eye of the storm gathering around two men who knew exactly who they were, and what had brought them here.

Crowe flicked dust from his coat with the polish of a man who'd done this before. He untied the duster, then let it fall. He holstered his revolver slow, making a show of calm he didn't fully feel.

"You always were too proud for your own skin," he said.

Cole drew a short breath, jaw tight, shoulders squared. "You whipped the wrong man."

Crowe's hand hovered near his holster. Cole's did the same.

The world shrank to heartbeats. Sunlight. Breath.

Then—

A shout. A silver flash of metal. A horse screamed in the distance.

Crowe drew.

Cole fired first.

The report blasted sharp, faster than the crowd could follow. Crowe staggered, hand jerking wide. His bullet flew wild, blew a hole through a church post behind Cole, and fell into the dust.

Crowe buckled, hand pressed to his chest where the bullet had struck hard and true. His eyes widened, full of that sharp disbelief men feel when death comes by a name they didn't think mattered.

He fell to his knees.

And Cole stepped forward—still gasping, still bleeding—and said the only words he had left:

"This town ain't yours anymore."

Crowe's fingers twitched once, like he might argue. Then they went still. His head hit the dirt, his eyes wide and lifeless.

The fighting died a moment later, like everyone had been waiting for the signal. The remaining gang members saw the truth in the street and dropped their weapons, some running for the hills, others simply standing—lost, leaderless, stunned.

* * *

Cole's gun slipped from his fingers.

It hit the dirt with a dull clatter just before his knees buckled, the last of his strength gone. His breath came in short, broken bursts, shoulders shaking as pain and relief warred.

Maggie was already running toward him. So was Reverend Holt. And then — as if some silent signal had passed through the crowd — half the town surged forward. Eben, the blacksmith. Widow Hensley. Clara Penrose. Nate Curry. Even children broke from their parents, wide-eyed and trembling.

They caught Cole just as he pitched forward. Maggie cradled his shoulders against her, the preacher steadying his back, his wounds bleeding.

"It's all right," Maggie breathed, her voice softer than it had been in days. "You did it, Cole. It's over. Crowe's gone."

Jesse pushed between them, face streaked with sweat and dust, eyes wide with something that was almost pride. In his hands was a tin cup of water.

"I got it — here—" Jesse said, dropping to his knees. His hands shook, but he held the cup steady as

235

he guided it toward Cole's parched lips. "Drink. C'mon — you gotta drink."

Cole's eyes opened enough to recognize him. And then he drank.

Not much. Just a swallow or two. But enough to steady him. Enough to prove he was still here.

The crowd hushed — not out of fear, but from recognition. They'd never seen a man stand that tall before falling. Never seen someone take on what they'd all felt powerless against — and win.

Holt leaned in, clasping Cole's hand in both of his, voice low but full of fire. "You gave them their courage back," he whispered. "And now you've given them their home."

Maggie shook her head, brushing sweaty hair from Cole's brow with trembling fingers. "No," she said. "He reminded them it was theirs all along."

Cole blinked. His chest rose, slow and cracked. His strength wasn't back yet — not even close — but something far greater than muscle steadied him now.

Relief. Freedom.
And the small, stubborn beginning of hope.

When Cole's head finally settled against Maggie's shoulder, Jesse leaned closer, still holding the dented cup.

"We'll get you home," he said, voice rough. "We ain't done yet."

And for the first time in a long while, the town of Copper Creek nodded in agreement.

Together.

* * *

The street lay quiet now, the dust beginning to settle. The acrid smell of gunpowder still lingered in the warm air, mingling with sweat and something else—relief, sharp and startling, like a lungful of clean air after too long underwater.

"Oh, Cole," Maggie whispered, voice breaking as tears finally came. "You stubborn, fool-hearted man."

He managed a smile—small, dry around the edges—and reached up with a shaking hand to brush a tear from her cheek. "I wasn't lookin 'to be a hero, Maggie."

"You weren't," Old Nate rumbled, limping up behind her, hat held in both hands. "But you went and did it anyway."

The preacher knelt beside them, laying a gentle hand on Cole's shoulder. "You bore the weight others

237

were too frightened to. Today, you've given them their voice again."

Clancy limped over, arm bandaged, one hand pressed tight to the wound Cole had warned him might kill him someday. He stood tall all the same. "That was one hell of a shot, Hardin," he said. "Glad I was here to see it."

Others gathered—faces familiar, newly brave, newly grateful. Women with kerchiefs and rifles in hand. Men with scraped knuckles and eyes still wide with the memory of their own defiance. And scattered through them all, the glances of children peeking out from behind their mothers, catching sight of the man whose stand had changed everything.

Cole drew a breath—a long, slow one—and felt it hitch with the pain across his ribs and back. "Ain't just me," he rasped. "You all did what mattered."

"Maybe," Maggie said, "but someone had to show us."

A few feet away, someone dragged Crowe's body off the street. No one flinched. No one said a word. It was done. The hold he'd had wasn't just loosened—it was broken.

The preacher rose and turned toward the people. "Let us tend to the wounded," he said. "Let us bury the dead. Let us cleanse this town from the stain it's carried too long."

And slowly—like dawn breaking over a black horizon—people began to move. Some to fetch water, some to fetch blankets, some just to reach out and take Cole's hand as they passed. He accepted each one with weary thanks, his arms trembling, his breath still uneven. But his eyes… his eyes were bright.

"You all right?" Maggie asked softly, brushing a lock of hair from his forehead.

Cole let out a slow, ragged laugh. "Used to think I was just passing through," he said. "Reckon that might've changed."

She squeezed his hand. "Copper Creek won't forget what you did here, Cole Hardin."

The church bell tolled then—once, twice—a sound not of mourning, but of beginning. Of something new. And as the sunlight broke through the clouds overhead, the town finally felt it:

Copper Creek belonged to its people again.

EPILOGUE:
A New Day in Copper Creek

The wind had changed.

It no longer carried the sharp edge of fear, but the slow, promising scent of woodsmoke, wild sage, and something else—something like peace. The scars of the last fight were still visible in Copper Creek: a few broken boards in front of Maggie's store, a bullet-scarred hitching post near the church, and a burned-out shed that no one seemed eager to rebuild just yet.

But there were new sounds too—laughter from the blacksmith's yard, the steady hammer of repairs on the livery, the rustle of children playing by the watering trough without looking over their shoulders.

And sitting on the porch of the boarding house, shirt unbuttoned to keep anything from scraping the wounds across his back, rested Cole Hardin.

He held a tin mug of coffee—good and strong—the kind Maggie had bullied him into drinking "unless he wanted to die just to spite her." His hair was still mussed on one side, jaw still purpled with bruises, but there was color in his cheeks again, and a steady light in his eyes.

Nate approached with a slow step and a louder sigh, cane tapping dusty boards. "Town's lookin 'better today," he said, settling down beside Cole. "Feels different too."

Cole nodded. "Ain't looked this free since I rode in."

"Ain't looked this free ever," Nate corrected, squinting at the street with something that almost looked like pride. "You think you might stick around and see what comes of it?"

Cole didn't answer right away. He watched a pair of boys run past, wooden rifles raised like heroes, calling out imaginary orders. He saw Maggie helping sweep the boardwalk next door, laughing when Jesse nearly dropped a barrel on his own boot. He saw the preacher, Bible in hand, chatting with Clancy's daughter about planting an almond tree by the church.

"Could be," Cole said quietly. "Could be I've got a stake in this place now."

Nate grunted. "Hell of a stake to earn, all things considered."

Cole's grin was lopsided. "That it is."

Maggie headed over just then, apron tied over a fresh calico dress, hair tucked up neat beneath a blue ribbon. "Aren't you supposed to be restin'?" she said, hands on her hips. "Coffee ain't rest, Cole Hardin. Doctor said bed."

Cole looked up at her, eyes shining soft. "Bed's overrated. This is where the world's happening."

She arched a brow. "You wanna add 'stubborn 'to those scars, that's your call." But her tone was warm, and she reached out to shake her head affectionately. "Just don't think Copper Creek's done with you yet."

From down the street, a horse neighed. Someone called for timber. The church bell rang midday, not as a warning, but a reminder.

Life was beginning again.

Cole leaned back, wincing only slightly, and let a quiet breath out, one he hadn't known he was holding.

"Yeah," he said. "Reckon it ain't done with me at all."

And with the sun warm on his face and the promise of a tomorrow he'd fought to earn, Cole Hardin finally let himself believe it.

That the worst was behind them.

And the best was theirs to build.